"With a sure hand and a steady heart, Laurel Mills charts a course from an ocean of sorrow into an eddy of hope. These vivid, seamless pages tell an elegant story."

—Abby Frucht, author of *Life Before Death* and *Polly's Ghost*

"In lean, effective prose, Laurel Mills has written a novel that uncovers the mystery of a death, and in the process, even greater mysteries about the human heart."

—Jonis Agee, author of *South of Resurrection* and *The Weight of Dreams*

Undercurrents

A NOVEL BY

LAUREL MILLS

RISING
TIDE
PRESS

Rising Tide Press
PO Box 30457
Tucson, AZ 85751-0457
520-888-1140

Printed in the United States on acid-free paper.

Publisher's note:
All characters, places, and situations in this book are fictitious, or
used fictitiously, and any resemblance to persons (living or dead) is
purely coincidental.

Cover art: Paula Deyoe

First Printing: October 2001

Mills, Laurel
Undercurrents

ISBN 1-883061-37-7

Library of Congress Control Number: 2001 132070

ACKNOWLEDGEMENTS

I wish to thank the Ragdale Foundation for providing a quiet and nurturing environment in which to write. I am also grateful to the University of Wisconsin-Fox Valley for grants that allowed me time to work on this manuscript. Thank you to Joan Hendry, Jackie Calhoun, Dawn Turner Trice, Laura Pritchett, Ellen Kort, Rusty McKenzie, Helen Fahrbach, Marge Higgins, Kay Saunders, Lisa Bay, Chris Miller, Barbara Bryant, Sandra Ingraham, and other writing friends for advice and support.

My appreciation to my editor, Laurie Field, and to my agent, Barbara Harris. A special thank you to Debra Tobin, Brenda Kazen, and all the women of Rising Tide Press.

My fond gratitude to my family for all our adventures along the Maine coast: Brad and Mary Lothrop; Sherryl Porter; Maureen and Butch Riggs.

Most of all, I am grateful to Lynn for her long and unwavering belief.

For Lynn Koss,

who graces my life

After what happened, I didn't think I'd ever come back to Maine, especially to Quarry Island. I wavered about making the trip—first I thought I would go, then I thought no, I'm not up to it. The lure of home, though, was too strong and in the end I just packed up and got in the car. Grace and I usually left the city on Memorial Weekend, when our teaching semesters ended. She'd administer finals for her American Lit classes at Boston University. I'd grade the portfolios of my photography students at the Art Institute. Then, both of us exhausted, we'd be on the road for Maine. But here it was the middle of June and I was just now heading north. Alone.

The tires complained to the highway under me. Trees along I95 whizzed by. I yanked off my silver feather-shaped earrings, and tossed them onto the dashboard. Those wouldn't be necessary where I was going. Rolling down the window, I was hit by a rush of pine-scented air as I slowed for the exit onto Route One in Brunswick and continued north. The narrow road was clogged with tourist traffic all the way up the coast, especially in Wiscasset where I had to wait a half an hour to get over the bridge.

I pulled into the waterfront in Rockland and was lucky to get a last minute ticket for the ferry. After parking my Escort near the bow, I climbed the stairs to the top deck. Rather than standing at the rail as Grace and I used to do, I found a place to sit on one of the benches. Slowly, the ferry pulled away. I looked down at the dock as we left, at the pilings coated with barnacles and seaweed.

Without thinking, my hand went to Grace's gold chain at my throat. Even these nine months after her accident, I still couldn't get used to the fact that the pendant on the chain was missing—a gold heart with a pearl set in it. As I fingered the chain, I thought about the spring afternoon just last year when I'd given the necklace to Grace. That day, the sky had been gray and dismal like today, misting off and on. We'd spent part of the morning at Fenueil Hall, then gone into the Durgin Park restaurant for lunch. At a long table, covered with a red-checkered cloth, we sat with a group of strangers and enjoyed the scallops and the insults of the waiters. Afterward, we strolled around Quincy Market and came across a street musician playing the guitar and singing *Mr. Bo Jangles*. I tugged on Grace's sleeve for her to stop, and we listened to the shaggy-haired performer, throwing a few quarters into his guitar case. After the song ended, I asked Grace to close her eyes, then placed the necklace around her neck and clasped it. Her green eyes darted with self-consciousness as she whispered, "Martha, one of my students is standing right over there." But for just a second, she laid her hand over mine as I patted the pendant into place in the hollow of her collarbone. Now, I gulped a couple of times as I yanked the zipper on my jacket, concealing the empty gold chain at my throat.

While the ferry moved through Penobscot Bay, I looked back at where I'd come from. My eyes drifted over the sea. The water seemed as gray as the sky. After almost a half-century of living near the Atlantic, I'd seen the ocean in every possible way. Sometimes it was flat and harmless-looking, even dull, like today. But the water was always so cold that if anyone fell in, he wouldn't survive long. Sometimes the fog rolled in so thick, you couldn't see a thing. Other times, the winds turned the ocean mean, smashing against the rocky shoreline.

The ferry plodded through a maze of tiny islands. After an hour, we moved into the Reach near Quarry Island, past granite ledges topped by spruce forests. There was no turning back now. I stood up from the bench and leaned against the rail as the ferry approached Hailey's Harbor, the pilot maneuvering the boat into its berth.

All the weeks I'd put off this trip, I had especially dreaded this moment. This was what Grace and I had liked most: arriving at the island, knowing we had the whole summer ahead of us. During our twenty years together, we'd always luxuriated in this landing.

I drove off the ramp and through the parking lot of the terminal. Turning left, I passed huge slabs of granite that lay abandoned, grass and wild flowers growing up around them. Granite Road snaked along the west end of the island.

I drove past Sue Whitaker's house and the medical clinic. Sue's huge cinnamon cat, Fat Alice, was sunning herself on the clinic steps. There wasn't any sign of Sue outside working in her flower gardens, so I assumed she was probably with a patient. Over this last winter, I'd talked with Sue on the phone nearly every week, but I hadn't told even her exactly when I was coming to Maine. Sue had been on the dock last fall when Jake brought Grace's body in, and I wasn't ready to face those memories.

Further along Granite Road, I neared Old Cove and approached my widowed brother's house. Should I stop and let Jake know I was on island? My nephew David—always full of childlike gusto—would be eager to see me. As I slowed, my eyes were drawn beyond the yard, past the meadow, further to the harbor. Jake's blue-and-white lobsterboat—*The Sybil*—sat on its mooring, floating calmly. The sun, which was beginning to burn through the gray sky, glinted off the brass coaming—a brass half-round strip on a raised board around the cockpit meant to prevent water from running into the boat. Even from this distance, it seemed to me I saw Grace's blood spattered on that brass strip.

Quickly, I turned my eyes away and rammed my foot on the gas pedal. I sped past Old Cove, leaving behind the house where I'd grown up.

Granite Road narrowed even more as I continued along the border of the island. At Seal Point I turned toward the sea, onto the sandy road that branched off to my cottage. Nailed to a birch tree and hanging a little crooked, a weathered board read *Martha Felkins / Grace O'Donnell.*

I parked in a flat spot where the grass was sparse and thin. It didn't seem possible, but everything was as it had always been. The lilac bushes had already lost their flowers, but the wine-colored peonies were beginning to bloom. As I sat in the car, reluctant to get out, I could tell that Jake had opened up the cottage. He kept an eye on it over the winter and opened it for me every spring. Of course, David must have helped him.

My nephew, who was now in his early twenties, had been diagnosed as brain damaged and trainable mentally retarded when he was a preschooler. Over the years, the name of his condition changed. For a while, *developmentally disabled* came into vogue, now *cognitively delayed* was the politically correct term. No matter what you called it, David was slow. We all felt protective toward him, like you would toward a child.

David was Jake's shadow. Everywhere that Jake went, David followed, especially after my sister-in-law, Sybil, died of leukemia four years ago. So if Jake had come over from Old Cove to open my cottage, David would've been here too.

I hadn't told Jake what day I'd be arriving, but he'd prepared the cottage anyway, just as he always did. Signs that he'd been caring for it were everywhere: windows shiny clean, firewood stacked along the side of the cottage. I knew the inside would be ready too: the gas and water turned on, the phone hooked up.

"Well, what am I waiting for?" I mumbled to myself. "Doesn't do any good to sit here all day." I leaned into the back seat to scoop up my camera bag and a paper sack of groceries.

On the steps to the screened-in porch, I paused with my hand on the latch of the screen door. A chipmunk scurried across the yard and dashed through the lattice under the porch. Gulls screeched down near the water, and the air was rich with the smell of pine trees and saltwater.

The screen door squeaked when I opened it. Right in front of me was Grace's favorite chair, the wicker rocker where she'd sat in the evenings, reading as the sun went down. I took off my jacket and wrapped it around the chair back. From the back where I stood, it almost looked as if a person were sitting in the chair. With a press of my foot at the tip of the rocker, it started to rock.

The daybed was in its usual place next to the inner wall,

a worn army blanket stretched over the lumpy mattress. When I sat down, the old springs sagged even though I'm tall and thin—Grace used to say my meat was close to the bones but sweet to eat. Dropping my deck shoes from my feet to the floor, I laid down and rested my head on the feather pillow, still musty from winter. This daybed on the porch was where Grace and I had first made love, the summer I first brought her to the island so many years ago. The gray sky that had threatened during the ferry ride was breaking up, and patches of sunlight shone through the screens. I imagined Grace's coppery hair in that light, imagined her lying here with me now.

Grace was everywhere.

I pushed myself off the daybed and slammed my feet into my shoes. It took several trips back and forth to unload the car. First, I brought in a rosewood box about the size of a shoebox with a hinged cover. The box was a wonderful reddish-brown color, was etched with an intricate design of interlocking seashells, and had a bronze latch. I set it on my bedroom dresser and draped Grace's gold chain over it.

After I'd carried in the luggage and groceries, I began the unpacking, taking the perishables out of the ice cooler and setting them in the fridge. The cardboard boxes of canned and packaged goods sat on the floor, waiting for me to tackle them next, but I felt too jittery to concentrate. I'd open a box and lift out a can of corn, then stand in the middle of the kitchen, holding the can in one hand, chewing the thumbnail of my other hand. After a while, I gave up on the unpacking and walked aimlessly from room to room, opening windows to let the stale air escape.

It wasn't like me to feel restless when I was on island. Grace and I always talked about how much we liked the peaceful feeling of being at the cottage. Now I felt uneasy.

Why had I come back? Being here made me miss Grace even more than in the city, though I'd never have thought that possible. My longing for her was a physical ache, a burning in my heart and gut. Wrapping my arms around my stomach, I leaned against the kitchen sink. Then I looked down at the white enamel.

How many times had I washed Grace's hair in this sink? Undoing her long braid. Lathering shampoo into her scalp, streaming water through her red hair.

Impulsively, I turned the faucet on full force and stuck my head under the water. It filled my ears, wetting my collar, drenching my shirt. I cried into the sink, the water running colder and colder.

Later, head still wet, I turned on a lamp in the living room and rummaged through the magazine shelf of the bookcase. I settled into an armchair and browsed through old issues of *Aperture, Art Journal, Image,* even Grace's *American Literature.* Several issues of *Down East* and *Yankee* contained my work, and I looked at those, thinking of how I'd shoot the photos if I were doing them now. I must have dozed because I came to with a start, knocking an open magazine off my lap. It was getting dark outside when I fixed a light supper of apple slices and sharp cheese.

In bed I tried to read, but my mind kept wandering and I'd read the same sentence two or three times. The room was too quiet—no night chatter, no arguments. I wanted Grace. Right now I'd give anything for a good fight. Anything, just to have her here.

Slipping a sweater over my nightgown, I stepped outside and sank into one of the Adirondack chairs. The weather was chilly, and the sky had cleared. I soon tired of watching the stars alone, so I snapped on the flashlight and carefully made my way down the path to the beach. I reached the cove, pulled the sweater tighter, wrapped my arms around myself, and leaned against the old boathouse where Grace and I stored our small fishing boat, outboard motor, poles, and tackle. I loved looking out over the sea, even at night, and listening to the surf as it lapped the shore.

Moving closer to the water line, I dug the toes of my shoes into the coarse sand. Soon the incoming tide began to wash over my shoes and splash against my ankles, but I still stood there.

I began to sing. Jake had always teased me that I could form a barbershop quartet with a shower pipe, a sea gull, and the diesel engine of his boat. Standing in the dark at the edge of the roaring surf, I started timidly. First, *Amazing Grace*. Next, Grace's and my love song, *The Rose*. I belted out the songs to no one: *Kumbaya, Blowin' in the Wind, Where Have All the Flowers Gone?* and *Puff the Magic Dragon*. Songs Grace had made up for David: *Ten Lobsters in a Trap* and *99 Bushels of Clams on the Shelf*. I sang what I could remember of *O Holy Night*.

As the tide came in, I stepped back, boulder by boulder. I felt foolish, my voice hoarse. The surf crashed against the rocks, salt spray stinging my cheeks and forehead.

Back at the cottage, I took off my wet clothes, changed into a dry nightgown, and climbed into bed. Then I drifted into a sound sleep.

In the nightmare, I wailed. It was that kind of dream where your mouth is stretched so wide it hurts, your throat is raw, and you're roaring, but only bits of sound are trickling out. My pitiful whimpering woke me.

I'd dreamt Grace was leaving me. I was on my knees begging her to stay, and she was walking down a long corridor, not even looking back. She flung her long red hair and stepped into an elevator. Then just before she disappeared, she turned and tried to tell me something.

"What are you saying?" I cried. "Louder! I can't hear you." Her lips moved in exaggerated slow motion, but I couldn't catch the words. Then the elevator closed, and she was gone.

It took sitting on the edge of my bed, shaking my head vigorously, to remember where I was. The salt air drifting in through the open window helped to orient me. The clothes I'd worn yesterday lay heaped on the wide-plank floor. I stepped into them, tossing the nightgown onto the rumpled bed.

To clear my mind of the dream, I threw myself into physical work, clearing winter debris from the flowerbeds. A stone fence ran along one side of the cottage, and I noticed that some of the stones had come loose. I wedged them back in place and chinked the gaps with moss.

While I was repairing some loose boards on the lattice around the porch, the phone rang. Jamming the hammer into the belt loop on my jeans, I dashed inside the house, and grabbed it on the fourth jingle.

"I wondered if you were back," Sue said. "Why didn't you call?"

It was good to hear her voice. Leaning against the kitchen counter, I said, "I just got in last night."

"I'm glad you're here. Hope you're up for some sailing this afternoon."

"Jeez, Sue," I laughed, "I'm not even unpacked yet."

"That can wait. Come on, Martha. I need someone to play with. Get me away from this clinic."

I started to protest until she said, "Since school got over, every kid on the island has been in. Poison ivy, ear infection, ringworm. You name it, I've seen it within the last few weeks. I figured I could count on you to rescue me from runny noses and rashy bottoms." Sue was the only doctor on Quarry Island, having replaced old Dr. Peterson. When she arrived, Grace and I were glad to welcome another middle-aged dyke to the island. We'd struck up a friendship that renewed itself each summer.

"I don't know," I said, scratching my back against the edge of the counter. "I'm not very good company these days."

"Meet me at the dock in about an hour."

"You're serious, aren't you?" I asked.

"You have something better to do?"

I freed the hammer from my belt loop, juggling it in one hand. I couldn't think of a single thing.

Sue was waiting for me at the Hailey's Harbor dock. Her frizzy hair stuck out over her sun visor, and she wore a navy blue sweater, white cotton slacks rolled up to the calf, and Topsiders. "Hey, I like your hair like that," she called out when she saw me.

I ran my fingers through my short hair. "It doesn't look too chopped off? Too butch?"

Sue laughed. "It's becoming. And I like the silver streaks. Lady Clairol?"

I groaned. "Mother Nature."

She gave me a warm hug, then held me at arm's length. "How are you, Martha? Really."

I felt my eyes tearing up, so I avoided her gaze. "I'm all right."

"Let's get out on the water." She squeezed my shoulders. "We can catch up with each other's news once we're under way."

It felt right to be walking down the catwalk to the floating dock where Sue's tender was tied up. She rowed out to her mooring where we boarded her twenty-five foot Friendship sloop, *Remedy*. It was my job to take off the sail cover while Sue opened the hatch and stowed our gear in the cabin. I raised the jib and hoisted the mainsail, and with Sue at the helm we sailed out of the harbor. It was a glorious late afternoon with a wind of four to seven knots. Sun reflected off the sea, green finger-like kelp and colorful lobster buoys bobbing on its surface. Seals flopped lazily on outcroppings of rocks, and a pair of porpoises rolled and surface-dived behind us.

Once out of the harbor, we ran with the wind. Sue handled the tiller. I worked the sails, cranking in lines with the winch handle and ducking the boom. We passed an island of terns on our port side. Off our stern, Clarence Potts was hauling a lobster trap onto the rail of his boat, and he waved to us.

We sailed for quite a while before Sue suggested gunkholing, anchoring in a secluded spot. Traveling along the shore, we searched for an isolated area, then let the main down and dropped anchor in a sheltered cove off Rock Island.

"God, it's great being on the water." I sat on the port bench, hugging my feet.

Sue stretched out in the starboard seat. "I'm glad to see you smiling."

The water felt cold and delicious as I trailed my fingers over the side. "I feel lighter than I have in a long time."

Sue applied sun block to her face. She didn't get it all rubbed in, and her nose was streaked with white lotion. "Are you sure you're all right, Martha?" she asked. "Managing okay without Grace?"

I swallowed hard before I answered. "The winter was a lot tougher than I thought it was going to be." I took the sun block from her and spread it on my arms and legs. "I tried to keep on the go so I wouldn't have time to think of her. Spent a lot of time on campus, working with students. And I'm preparing for an exhibit. But you can't fill up every minute, even in the city where there's so much going on. What fun is it to go to concerts or the theater, or do anything, without her? Even when I'm with friends, there's a huge hole in my life. Sitting down to the dinner table alone, crawling into bed alone, that's hard."

Sue shielded her eyes from the sun and looked over at me. "What about now? Are you finding it any easier on island?"

"Last night, I could hardly stand it—Grace not being with me. Didn't sleep much." I set the tube of sun block on the bench and hugged my knees again, resting my chin on my knees. "It'll get better—there's plenty to keep me busy this summer."

"With the cottage?"

I nodded. "There's always something that needs fixing."

Sue climbed down the hatch to the cabin, then brought up a small cooler of Miller Lite sitting in crushed ice. She opened a bottle for each of us, and we clinked them together. "To summer and strong women," Sue said. I couldn't help but smile. We drank the cold beer and shared a bag of vinegar potato chips while Sue told me about a medical conference she'd recently attended in San Francisco. She'd come away feeling invigorated after five days of discussions with other family physicians; she said it helped allay the isolation she sometimes felt as an island doctor. We each cracked open another bottle—the chips made us thirsty— and I talked about my photography. The Guild of Boston Artists had invited me to hang some photos for an exhibit by area art professors, scheduled to open in the fall. It felt good to discuss my vision for the show. After a while, the sun overhead made us sleepy and we stretched out on our individual seats and dozed, the *Remedy* lolling peacefully in the gentle waves, water lapping its hull.

It was late afternoon by the time Sue sat up and asked, "Ready to head back? Maybe catch a bite to eat in town?"

"In a minute. There's something I've been meaning to ask you." I'd been awake for the last ten minutes, my mind working a puzzle that had bothered me all winter.

"Shoot." Sue swung her feet onto the deck.

I pushed myself into a sitting position and set my feet on the deck. My back was full of kinks from lying on the hard bench, and I rubbed my hips. "About Grace's accident," I said. "I never did quite understand how she died."

As we sat facing each other, Sue took time to re-adjust her visor. She seemed to be mulling over how to say it to me. Her words were gentle when she explained, "There was a laceration on the back of her scalp. That's where the bleeding came from. The autopsy showed that death was due to dislocation of the neck. When she fell she must have struck her head, causing that cut and snapping the vertebra."

I'd read that on the death certificate, but I hated hearing it out loud. And it still didn't make sense to me. I wrapped my arms around my chest. "But why would she fall? I mean, on Jake's boat? And how was that fall enough to kill her?"

Sun glinted on the brass fittings of *Remedy*, and the ocean we floated on seemed dark and mysterious. "Jake told us she came down hard," Sue said. "She must have hit the base of her head on the washboard, and snapped her neck on the coaming."

"Is that possible?"

"Well, it was freaky, I admit." Sue lifted the empty blue

cooler from the deck and dumped the melted ice over-board. There was the sound of water spilling into water. "Think about it, though, Martha. That edge around the cockpit is raised, what, maybe two inches from the gun-wale? That's enough right there, if she hit just right. But then there's that brass strip along the edge. When her neck slammed against that, with the force of her falling . . ."

"That's what I don't get," I persisted. "What made her fall? I mean, Grace was always sure-footed. She had good balance. And it wasn't as if she'd never been on a boat before. I just can't picture her going down like that."

"The deck must have been slippery," Sue replied patiently as she fit the plastic cover on the cooler. "Jake and David had been hauling traps, and you know how wet and slimy the deck can get. And if Jake got side-swiped by an unexpected swell the way he said he did . . ."

"Even that seems strange. He's such an experienced cap-tain. Why didn't he anticipate the swell and turn into it?"

"Maybe he was distracted by something." Sue reached over and put her hand lightly on my knee. "The autopsy indicated a broken neck. That kind of injury could be explained by Grace's fall. But I don't know *why* she fell. Martha, if you were really concerned, maybe you should have asked more questions at the inquest."

"I was in such a state of shock at the time, I hardly remembered my own name or what day it was. But since then, I don't know, something just doesn't seem quite right."

"I think you're worrying for no good reason," Sue said as she squeezed my knee affectionately. "Accidents are hard to accept—they happen so suddenly and we're unpre-pared to deal with them emotionally. You've lost your part-ner and best friend. It's hard to deal with such a loss. Give it more time."

"I suppose you're right. I'm probably making a mountain out of a molehill," I said as Sue prepared to lift anchor. I raised the sails, wondering if there ever were satisfactory answers to the questions that bothered us most.

We skimmed back toward the harbor, the breeze bellying the sails, *Remedy* heeling into the wind. On one of the tiny islands we passed, several black cormorants were holding out their wings, drying them. An osprey dove into the sea and came up with an alewife. For a while, a seal swam alongside the boat, its head just above the water, its soulful eyes watching us.

As we got closer to the mouth of the harbor, Sue said, "We're going to do one more tack, then we're going to bear away and head in."

At Sue's mooring, we secured *Remedy*, cleating and coiling the lines. We furled the sails, covered the main, then climbed into the tender and rowed to the dock.

Supper was spent leisurely at the Seagull's Nest. I didn't say anything more about Grace's accident. There was a guitar player at one end of the restaurant, singing Fifties songs. We kept making requests, calling out the names of old songs. Sue asked for *Ain't Nothing But a Hound Dog* but when the guy tried to swivel his hips like Elvis, we got the giggles. He was bald and must have weighed three hundred pounds. It felt good to laugh, and we were in no hurry to leave. Around ten o'clock, the guitar player quit so we paid our bill and left. Sue went on to her house next to the clinic, and I drove back to my cottage.

Again that night, I had trouble sleeping. I'd hoped that after the relaxing afternoon on the water and the pleasant supper with Sue, I'd drop right off. But when I got into bed and turned off the lamp, my eyes stayed wide open, staring at the bare wood ceiling. I kept thinking about the discussion we'd had about Grace's death. Maybe Sue was right—the deck was slippery, she lost her footing, and hit her head. It was as simple as that. The accident happened just like Jake told us.

The moon shone through the window, its light playing faintly on the ceiling and walls, changing patterns as clouds passed over the edges of the moon. These shifting outlines conjured up memories of Grace teaching David to make shadow puppets. She was so patient with him as she showed him how to throw the shapes of ducks or dinosaurs onto the wall with his hands.

Whenever he stayed over with us, she would be the one to tuck him into bed at night. We kept a small bedroom just for him, with a single maple bed, a scuffed-up maple dresser that had more matchbook cars than clothes in the drawers, and a desk stuffed with crayons and coloring books.

Grace would sit on the edge of David's bed and tell him a story of a fox chasing a rabbit, illustrating the tale by making silhouettes with her hands. The bunny won every time, sneaking into the corner of the wall where the fox shadow could not catch him. Grace was always the one to give David his last kiss goodnight. Sometimes I lingered in the doorway and listened to her stories, then I'd see her bend over and put her lips on his forehead, David's eyes squeezed tight, a happy smile on his face.

In an effort to shut out this memory, I rolled over on my side and punched my pillow, bunching it under my head. But my mind wouldn't let up thinking about Grace. Something about her accident was like those shifting moon shadows on the wall. Something kept slipping out of shape.

CHAPTER 2

The alarm clock read six a.m. Today would have been Grace's birthday. I shuffled in my slippers out to the kitchen. While I was waiting for the kettle to boil, I stared out the window over the sink. It didn't seem right that the morning appeared so normal. The sun was in its place in the blue sky. Beyond the lilac bushes, the sea was nearing low tide like it did every twelve hours. How strange, that everything just kept moving on.

I carried a cup of tea out to the screened porch and sat in Grace's wicker chair. A squirrel clattered across the roof. As I sipped my tea, I thought about phoning Jake and David. Not now. Maybe later in the day, after I got settled in.

The unpacking didn't take very long once I got at it. I dumped the contents of the suitcase on the bed and then put the clothes away, hanging the long-sleeved blouses, jeans, and cotton slacks in the closet. I set my fisherman's knit sweater, an old cardigan, and a couple of sweatshirts on the closet shelf, and dropped sneakers and deck shoes on the floor. The rest went into the dresser: a pile of T-shirts, some shorts, my bathing suit, underwear and socks, two sleeveless nightgowns. Usually the dresser was stuffed with Grace's clothes too. Now, with just the few clothes I'd brought with me, it was half-empty.

As I shoved in the bottom drawer, an object wedged behind the dresser caught my eye. With the hook of a hanger, I pulled out Grace's old canvas fishing hat, coated with dust bunnies. I slapped it against my leg and sent the dust flying. Coughing and sneezing, I straightened the brim and punched the crown to get it back into shape. I turned the hat around and around in my hands before I hung it on the dresser mirror.

When I stepped back, I could see the hat itself and its reflection in the wavy glass. On top of the dresser sat the rosewood box with the gold chain draped over it. These, too, were doubled by their reflection in the mirror. Everywhere I looked, Grace looked back.

I needed to get out of that room. Sweat and hard work, being outdoors—that's what I needed. Clamming.

In no time at all I'd driven into the village and come back with a license. I gathered a rake, growth ring, and hod from the back storage area of the cottage. Outfitted in boots and gloves, and a hat against the sun, I was ready.

Instead of taking the ledge path down to my cove, I walked south along the high shoreline for a quarter of a mile, then followed a trail that sloped down toward a marshy bay. After a while, the path leveled and ran into sea grass. I pulled up my hip boots and picked my way through the long wet grass, black muck squishing over the toes of my boots. As I neared the flats, the musty salt-and-kelp smell assaulted my nose. A glistening expanse of mud stretched between the tidemarks.

On the flats, I stomped around to get the clams to spit.

Wherever I saw tiny holes, I knew there would be clams underneath. Bent over, I dug with the short-handled rake, then lifted the muck and dropped the mound near my feet. My first clam of the season! It was like finding a pearl in an oyster.

I worked with my body bowed over, head down, creating mounds as I dug. It was a backbreaking job, lifting the heavy mud in search of elusive clams, the sun beating down. Slowly, I moved along the flats, dragging the clam hod—a slatted wood basket that became heavier as I filled it. Only clams measuring at least two inches by the growth ring were keepers, but I was getting a decent haul. After several hours of working with my back curved, I straightened and shifted the kinks from my spine.

The tide was turning when I left the mudflats. Overhead, the sun was relentless as I walked to the cottage. The trip seemed longer going back than it had coming. Even half-full, the hod was heavy. But it felt good to be physically worn out.

A water hose lay coiled near the outside faucet, and I sprayed the mud from my boots and gloves, then spread them on the grass to dry.

Inside, standing at the kitchen sink in my bare feet, my pants legs rolled up, I washed the clams thoroughly. I let the cold water run on them for a while, then set them in a bed of kelp in the refrigerator.

A hot shower rinsed off the musty smell of the mudflats and eased the pain in my back. After lunch, I drove again into the village of Hailey's Harbor.

"I'm looking for birthday candles," I told the stock boy at Parson's Grocery. "One of those little boxes of candles for a cake."

The blond teenager, probably summer help, had his back to me and was shelving Del Monte peaches. Without turning around, he said, "Third aisle, by the confectioner's sugar." Gripping a utility knife in his right hand, he yanked across a cardboard box and slit it open.

"I looked there already, but the hook was empty. You seem to be all out."

The stock boy set the blade on the carton, turned around, and rubbed his palms on his apron. "I'll go in back and check."

"I'd really appreciate it."

"This is all I could find," the boy said when he returned, holding a dusty box of yellow birthday candles. The little plastic window was torn, and the color on the wax was streaked and fading.

"Oh, they're ugly, aren't they? Well, they'll have to do, I guess." I set the box in the cart and squeezed down the narrow aisle to the checkout at the front of the store.

Harry Parsons rang up the purchases. "Good to see you, Martha. Didn't know if you'd be back this summer."

"I wasn't sure either, Harry. But here I am." I handed him a twenty.

He packed the groceries into a paper bag. "Godawful sorry about Grace. We'll miss her," he said as he pushed the bag toward the edge of the counter.

I couldn't answer—just nodded. I picked up the bag with both hands and hurried out of the store, the bell over the door tinkling behind me.

I'd just placed the cake in the oven when the phone rang. Jake's voice sounded far away and muffled, though his house was only a mile-and-a-half down the road.

"Martha, when did you get here?"

"Just a few days ago," I said, pulling out a chair from the table and sitting down. "I was going to call you but just hadn't got around to it yet."

"Getting settled in?"

"More or less. Thanks for opening the cottage. It was nice to have it ready when I arrived."

"Didn't take much time. David helped."

I rested my elbows on the table. "How is David?"

"He's watching television. That show he likes, *Let's Make a Deal*."

"And I bet he's yelling 'come on down!' right along with the TV."

Jake chuckled. "Ayuh. He's yelling, all right."

I crossed my legs and leaned back in the chair. "When are you and David coming over?"

"Later today. We came in off the water early. Fishing's poor this time of year."

"Why don't you come for supper?"

"That'd be good by me. Around five, five-thirty? We're headed downstreet first to get a few things. Need anything?"

"Not really. I just got back from Parsons, and I picked up some groceries. Wait, I guess I could use ice cream for dessert. Just a quart. Whatever flavor David likes. And a newspaper. I forgot to get one. A *Boston Globe* if you can find it."

"The book store carries lots of papers, far as I can remember. Anything else?"

"Does David have any Swiss chard in his garden?"

"Just starting to get some. I'll have him cut you a mess."

I suppose it was just habit, my baking that cake. I always baked one for Grace's birthday—she liked marble cake with chocolate frosting. My birthday came just a few days after hers, so we usually celebrated them at the same time, and that way one cake would do for both.

While the cake was cooling, I whipped up some frosting. Once the layers were covered, I positioned the yellow candles. As I cleaned out the frosting bowl and licked the knife, I thought *those wimpy candles don't look so bad after all.*

I didn't hear Jake's pickup truck pull into the yard, so the squeak and banging of the screen door startled me. David called, "Auntie Marfa? Where you at?"

Shoving the cake to the back of the counter, I answered, "David, I'm right here." I hurried out and met him on the porch.

He was wearing a green work shirt, and one button was missing so that it gaped over his round belly, his white T-shirt showing. His work pants were long for his short legs, and they dragged over the backs of his work boots. A floppy red felt hat was pulled down over his patchy brown hair. David's brown eyes lit up when he saw me, and he grinned and grabbed me in a bear hug, nearly lifting me off the floor. "Happy see you, Marfa," David said.

"I'm really glad to see you too," I answered, kissing him on the cheek. David clung to me as I reached behind him to open the porch door for Jake. My brother, at fifty-two, was a small but muscular man. We'd always been about the same height. Even with summer coming on, he wore a plaid flannel shirt with the sleeves rolled up, showing thermal underwear that covered his wiry arms.

I held the door open, and Jake looked up at me as he climbed the steps. "Jesus, you have a run-in with a boat prop? Your hair's shorter than mine," he said in way of greeting.

"Yeah, and getting to be as gray," I said, letting the screen door close behind him.

"We'll, sis, I guess we can thank our stars we ain't bald yet," Jake chuckled as he set a quart of Hood ice cream and a bread-bag full of Swiss chard on the wicker stand. He held up a rolled newspaper. "For the life of me, I couldn't find the *Globe*. They was all outta the *Portland Press Herald* too. So I figured you'd want *The Bangor Daily* instead. That do?"

"Sure, thanks." I carried the ice cream into the kitchen and put it into the freezer. When I came back, I unwrapped the Swiss chard. "This looks wonderful," I said. "It's so tender when the leaves are small like this. David, you did a good job growing this in your garden."

"Yep," he said over his shoulder as he headed into the cottage.

I turned to Jake. "I thought we could fix some potatoes and steamed clams with the chard for supper."

"You been clamming already?" Jake asked.

While I told Jake about my morning on the flats, David walked through the cottage and checked all the rooms. I could hear him clumping through the kitchen, living room, the small bedroom he used when he slept over, Grace's and my bedroom, even the bathroom. When he came back onto the sun porch, his brow was wrinkled and he looked confused. "Where Gracie at?" he asked.

Stunned by the unexpected question, I sagged against Jake. He didn't seem sure what to do, but he let me lean on him, his hands clumsily patting my back. "David don't mean nothing," he said. "What happened to Grace slipped his mind, is all. You know how he was when his mother died. Kept asking for her for months after."

David leaned into my face. "Marfa, you okay?"

I pushed myself away from Jake. "I'm okay. You don't need to worry."

"Gracie blow candles," David said.

"What in damnation?" Jake remarked.

Spotting a smudge of chocolate frosting on David's chin, I explained to my brother, "He must have found the cake I made."

"A cake? With candles and all? Don't tell me you made a birthday cake for Grace?"

When I didn't answer, just kind of dropped my eyes from his, Jake said, "Why in hell did you do that?"

"It's my birthday, too, in a few days. I made it for myself."

"Ayuh, sure you made it for yourself. What's the date today?"

"June seventeen."

"I believe that's Grace's birthday. Yours ain't until the twentieth, if I remember right." Shaking his head, Jake turned to his son. "David, look boy, don't you remember what I told you? Grace is gone. Remember Papa telling you she went away?"

David wrenched free from his father. "Her die?"

I sank into the wicker rocker and stared blankly out toward the sea. I hadn't known how David was going to react to Grace's being gone, but I hadn't expected this.

Jake sat down on the daybed, pulling David down beside him. "That's right, pal. Grace died. Like Mama did. You ain't gonna see Grace any more, just like you don't see Mama any more."

David looked puzzled. He twisted a strand of his hair and chewed the skin near his thumbnail. "I want see Gracie." He rocked his upper body rapidly back and forth. "Her come back!"

Jake grabbed David's arm to stop him from rocking. "Now, quiet down. We can't change it in any way, shape, or form. That's just the way it is. Grace is gone."

David kept rocking erratically. "Ohnn, ohnn, ohhn," he whined, a little patch of spittle pooling at the corner of his mouth.

"That's enough now!" Jake took hold of David's shoulders and turned him. "Look at me. I said quiet down. No more of this damn foolishness."

I picked up a picture book from the bottom shelf of the wicker stand and held it out. "David, remember this book? You always liked the red trucks in this book. Why don't you look at it while I get supper ready?"

He dropped his hands to his side and let up a little on his rocking, but his eyes were still troubled.

"Here, you take it." I set the book in his lap, opening it to a full-color photo of a fire truck. I tapped the page. "Remember when we saw a truck like this in Rockland?"

I made a motion with my head, and Jake got up and followed me into the kitchen.

"Sorry, sis," he said when we got out of David's hearing.

I leaned on the table with both hands, shaking my head slowly. Then I stood back and crossed my arms, clasping my shoulders. "It's just so hard, being here without Grace. And then David asks for her."

"He don't understand." Jake turned away and stared out the window. "We've all gotta get used to her being gone."

"I better hide this." I shoved the cake further back on the counter, behind the breadbox. "Maybe David will forget about it."

"Why'd you make that damn thing anyway?" Jake asked. "I mean, I can see a cake, but candles and the whole shebang?"

My hand lingering on the chrome refrigerator handle, I said, "I don't know, Jake. I can't explain it."

"Well, it don't matter," he said, his voice softening. "What do you say we get supper started?"

I scrubbed red potatoes and washed the chard, while Jake put clams in the steamer and set it on the stove.

Leaning against the enamel sink, Jake shook a cigarette out of the pack of Marlboros he carried in his shirt pocket. I noticed there was more white hair in his crewcut and deeper lines in the skin around his eyes than last year. He struck a kitchen match on the edge of the sink; ever since the time he found David playing with his Zippo lighter, he'd used a match to light his cigarette. He took a deep drag and said, "Did I tell you Owen Tuttle retired? Him and Emily been gone all winter, living in a trailer park in Florida. Their boy Jerry's in Atlanta now, and I guess they figured to be closer to him. I got an idea they'll move there for good."

"Do you think they'll keep the house here?"

"Doubt it." Jake knocked his ashes into the sink. "They got a high school kid living in it this summer. Owen hired him to paint the house, get it spruced up in case they decide on selling."

I set an ashtray on the counter. "Is it that same young man who painted their garage last summer? Bill? Or Brett? No . . . Ben, I think. Ben something or other."

"Don't know the kid's name, but I suppose that's the one." Jake ignored the ashtray and snubbed out his cigarette under the kitchen faucet, then dropped it into the sink.

"If it's the same boy, Grace and I ran into him a couple of times when he was at the Tuttle's last summer." Picking up the soggy butt, I tossed it into the garbage can. "Tall, blond kid? Shy? Kind of thin?"

"Couldn't say. He's been living in the Tuttle house a few weeks now, but I ain't seen much of him." Jake scooped some steamed-open clams into a bowl for David, then put that and an empty bowl for shells on the table. "David, come eat now!"

David lumbered into the kitchen and plopped down in a chair. I set a cup of melted butter by his place and said, "Be careful, it's hot. Do you remember how to get the clams out of the shells?"

"I do it," David assured me.

As I watched him, I thought about what a difficult time David used to have shucking steamed clams. He had learned easily enough to pull the clam free from the shell, but then he'd dip the clam into melted butter and shove the whole thing into his mouth without removing the black membrane that fit like a hood over the neck.

Grace had been the one to teach him the right way to shuck clams. She'd stood behind him at the table, put her arms around him, and used her hands to guide his. "See, David, it's like a man wearing a hat. Before we eat the man, we have to take off his hat. Like this . . ." and she'd helped him slip off the black membrane. David had loved Grace's story and never again needed help with steamed clams.

David ate his plate of clams and had seconds. With a buttery grin, he cleared the table, and Jake washed the dishes while I made coffee. When everything was put away, I scooped out dishes of ice cream that we carried to the porch. David ate his bowl, gripping his spoon like a shovel, and finished mine too. He seemed to have forgotten the cake I'd hidden.

Then, as he and Jake were leaving, David gave me a wet kiss on the cheek and asked, "Gracie come tomorrow?"

The cake sat on the seat beside me as I drove to Sue's. It looked pretty dreadful. There was a bare spot in the frosting where David had swiped it with his finger, and little holes dotted the top where the yellow candles had been.

I parked in the driveway of Sue's house, a small Cape Cod next to the medical clinic. Fat Alice, intent on a mission, was moving stealthily in the ferns at the side of the house. When the cat heard me drive in, she turned to look in my direction. A dead mouse dangled in her mouth. "Good for you, Fat Alice," I said through the windshield. "You still got what it takes." She lowered her head, her shoulders rolling under her fur, and disappeared in Sue's flower garden.

Carrying the cake, I poked the doorbell with my elbow. "Have you eaten dessert yet?" I asked when Sue opened the door.

"I was just about to cut into a pecan pie Sarah Atkins baked me for convincing her mother-in-law to go into a nursing home." She pulled me in and shut the door behind us. "Old Mrs. Atkins was living with them, and Sarah had all the care of her. With three kids too, she was getting exhausted."

"Pecan pie will keep. Eat this with me." I handed her the cake.

She held it out in front of her and looked at it quizzically. "Somebody sit on it?"

"Not exactly." I explained that I'd baked the cake because it was Grace's birthday and Jake thought that was a ridiculous thing to do.

"It's Grace's birthday? I'd forgotten," Sue said. "Are you okay?"

"Yeah. I just want someone to eat this damn cake with me."

"You're on." Sue set the cake in the middle of the living room floor. She plumped floor pillows on either side of it and patted one of them. "Sit here. I'll be right back."

I kicked off my shoes and sat yoga style on the pillow. An Enya CD was playing on the stereo, and a pair of candlesticks burned on the fireplace mantle. Already I felt better.

Sue came back carrying two bottles of Poland Spring water, napkins, and forks. She put these on the hearth, and was about to sit down when Fat Alice meowed at the front door. As Sue got up to let her in I said, "Careful. She might have a present for you."

I was glad to see that the cat had disposed of her prize outside. With a satisfied feline gait, she made a steady beam for the other floor pillow. She was about to settle in when Sue nudged her. "Move it, Alice. That's my spot." Arching her back indignantly, the cat jumped up on the sofa. Sue dropped onto the pillow, folding her legs under her. It wasn't long before Fat Alice slithered down and curled on the edge of the pillow at her side.

Sue handed me a fork. "Okay, dig in."

I took the utensil, but then set it on the napkin in my lap. "Shouldn't we do something for Grace first?"

"What?" Sue held her fork poised over the cake.

I felt foolish and could sense my cheeks burning. "Oh, nothing. It was a silly idea. Forget it."

"Wait a minute." Sue reached behind her and grabbed a newspaper from a basket. She spread it on the floor and smoothed it. Deftly, she folded several sheets into a pirate hat, which she placed on my head. Then she made one for herself and put it on. She took a burning candlestick from a silver holder on the mantle, and stuck it into the top of the cake. From behind the sofa, she fetched her guitar. By then, Fat Alice had taken over the floor pillow. When Sue lifted the edge of it, dumping her onto the floor, the cat complained with a series of cries. Sue settled again onto the cushion, feet tucked under her. "Ready?" she asked and when I nodded, she hit a note on the strings. We sang *Happy Birthday* as loudly as we could, with Fat Alice growling from the sofa. Then Sue and I ate the cake, right off the platter.

CHAPTER 3

M y own birthday—the big fifty—came sooner than I was ready for it. Half a century seemed such a milestone, but I wasn't up to celebrating it without Grace.

A few years earlier we'd marked her fiftieth. Sue and I had taken Grace to dinner at a nice restaurant in Camden, and we all wore long black skirts, shawls, and white wigs. We'd carried canes and walked stooped over, and Sue even had a little cigar she puffed on. I'll never forget the look on Grace's face when she tore the wrapping off her gift—at the dinner table while we were drinking coffee—and it was a box of Depends.

If Grace were around now she'd cook up something outrageous for my fiftieth. Drape the cottage in black crepe or something. But now, as I'd explained to Sue, I didn't really feel like making a big deal out of it.

I was expecting Jake to drop by that day. He'd called the night before and told me, "David's got a card he made for you. We'll stop over when we get in from tending pots."

In the late afternoon, I worked in the bathroom, patching the caulking around the bathtub. I was concentrating on trying to get a straight bead between the tub and the wall when a loud noise startled me. It seemed to be coming from outside. A strange sound: hysterical laughter, hiccuping, yelping.

Suddenly, I knew it was David.

David had made that same noise the time he'd uncovered a mole's nest with the lawnmower and tiny pink babies were spit out with the grass clippings. He'd made that sound the day of his mother's funeral four years ago. And the day of Grace's accident last September.

I dropped the caulking gun onto the bathroom floor and ran outside. David was standing about fifty feet in front of the cottage near where the land became rock and sloped steeply to the sea. He was stooped forward, his arms curled around his stomach, his eyes staring blankly. He must have dropped a piece of red construction paper, because it was fluttering on the ground, blowing toward me. I didn't stop to pick it up.

Rushing over to him, I called, "David! What is it?" But he kept staring vacantly, those terrible sounds coming from his mouth. Finally, I had to shake him by the shoulders to get him to look at me. I was not sure by the dazed look in his eyes that he knew me. But then he turned toward the sea, and as I followed his gaze I caught a glimpse of my brother.

"Jake!" I yelled, but he disappeared. I ran to where the ledges sloped and saw him scrambling down the footpath. Leaving David on the top of the cliff, I followed Jake. When I reached the cove, I saw thin swirls of red on the pebbly beach and screamed again, "Jake?"

"Quick, come here! Help me with this." I watched where he was moving to and saw a body sprawled on the shore. As I got closer I could see that it was a teenage boy (I'd guess around the age of seventeen or eighteen). As I reached the body, I thought I recognized him. He looked like the boy who'd painted the Tuttle's garage last summer.

His eyes had rolled back in his head, and his blond hair lay plastered to his forehead from the waves washing up against him. His left wrist had a deep gash across it, blood spurting from it.

As Jake leaned over him, I cried, "What's he done?"

Squatting next to the boy, Jake grabbed the limp arm, and pressed his fingers across the open wound, his thumb against the back of the wrist, making a vise to clamp off the bleeding. "I think the sonofabitch might of done it himself. Goddamn foolish kid. The knife's laying right there next to him." Sure enough, dropped into the wet tangle of kelp and periwinkle was a bloody fisherman's filet knife.

Jake's voice grew urgent. "Gotta stop this bleeding! Tear off a piece of my shirt. Hurry," Jake barked, "we need a bandage to pack this cut." Jake shrugged his free arm out of the sleeve of his flannel shirt. "Rip off a hunk there." He gestured with his head toward the shirt hanging from his shoulder.

Grabbing the fabric, I ripped a long piece of cloth up the back.

Jake said, "Fold it up and stick it under my fingers." The blood was leaking out under Jake's hand like a small river onto the beach.

I folded the green-plaid cloth and wedged it between Jake's hand and the wound. The boy seemed to be slipping in and out of consciousness, and once I thought I heard him moan, "Let me die."

"You take over now, Martha. I'll go for help. Here, press on this." Jake took his hand away from the wound and I replaced it with my own, pushing against the wad of cloth over the wrist. Already blood was oozing into the bandage.

"That's it," Jake said. "Keep the pressure there. And try to keep his arm up higher than his heart."

I nodded and tightened my grasp on the boy's bandaged wrist.

"Keep your eye on him," Jake said, quickly wiping his bloody hands on his workpants. As he sprinted toward the footpath, he yelled over his shoulder, "I'll check on David and use your phone to call Sue and Chancey."

I waited alone, squatting on my heels as I pressed on the wound. So much blood. My mind flashed back to Grace's accident. After what we'd gone through with her—this was just too much. I pushed harder against the open cut, trying to stop the bleeding. Could Jake be right? Did he cut himself on purpose? "Oh, you stupid stupid boy," I whispered, looking down at him.

I noticed his green-tinged lips, the dark circles under his eyes, a mole near his eyebrow. He looked so young and vulnerable. He wasn't even as old as David, I realized. His fingers were beginning to lose color, turning white. I wished Jake would get back. Wished he would bring help right away. Blood splattered a wild pattern over the boy's polo shirt, and his jeans were wet where the surf licked at his legs. Tightening my fingers on his wrist, I felt blood seeping through the cloth bandage. "You'll be fine," I said. But he wasn't fine at all.

By the time Jake and David came scurrying down the ledge, the piece of flannel cloth around the boy's wrist was saturated. David hung back, but Jake rushed right over to us. "Thank God, you're here," I said.

Jake knelt beside me and took over, pressing on the wound. "I got it now," he gasped, winded. "Go see to David."

When I let go and stood up, my legs were wobbly. David stood several feet from us, still making that wild half-laughing, half-crying sound. He'd lost his hat. His thin hair was blowing, his nose running, his shoulders shaking violently. I wiped my bloody hands on my jeans and put my arms out and held him so tightly I could feel the rapid thump of his heart.

Before long, sirens from Sheriff Chancey's police jeep and the island ambulance shrieked from Granite Road. David squeezed his eyes shut and threw his hands over his ears. I looked up to see the sheriff standing at the top of the cliff, flanked by the volunteer ambulance driver Harold Bryant, and Sue clutching her black doctor's bag.

Sheriff Chancey ran down the ledges, the holster on his belt bobbing up and down, his brown uniform stretching across his big belly. Sue followed, with Harold hurrying behind her carrying a rolled-up stretcher under his arm.

Sue leaned over the boy, listening to his heart and lungs with a stethoscope. "He's not an island kid," she said as she examined his eyes, noting the dilation of his pupils. She pressed two fingers on his neck to get his pulse, then quickly tore off some gauze and began wrapping his wounded wrist. "Do you know him, Jake?"

"Not at all. Could be that kid Owen Tuttle hired for the summer."

"I think his name might be Ben," I called to her. Just then, David opened his eyes and began to laugh hysterically. "Shhh," I said while I cradled him. "Shh, shhh." I watched while Jake and Harold and Chancey loaded the boy onto the stretcher and struggled to carry him up the footpath.

As she rushed by us, Sue yelled, "You and David okay, Martha?" When I nodded, she hurried after the stretcher.

After a short while, Jake rushed back down the path and joined me, now completely out of breath. "They're taking the kid to the airfield," he explained. "Sue's gonna fly with him over to the hospital so she can keep pressure on that wound and keep checking his blood pressure and pulse. Says she ain't sure how much blood he's lost." Jake placed his hands on David's shoulder and pried him from me. "Come on, boy," he said softly. "Let's you and me get on home. Everything's taken care of here."

I tried to hide my sudden trembling from Jake; I knew he wanted to get David home in his own familiar surroundings to calm him down. "Go," I insisted. "I'll be okay."

But after I watched them climb the footpath up the ledges, I thought *this is how I left the island last September*. Sinking to my knees, I vomited on the beach. Then, wiping my mouth with the back of my hand, I sat on my heels and looked out over the sea, wondering why I had come back.

The next day, in my mind I kept seeing that poor young man, crumpled on the beach, bleeding from that awful gash in his wrist. I tried to blot it out, tried to keep my brain from thinking about it. The job of caulking around the bathtub occupied me for a while as I worked on finishing it. But my hands shook and I made a mess of it, the line of caulk all squiggly instead of smooth, so I quit.

I wasn't going to forget it, so I might as well just deal with it. I hung my camera bag over my shoulder and headed out the door, back toward the scene of yesterday's trauma.

At the beach, I stopped and leaned against the side of the boathouse. The appalling event played over again in my mind: the boy's eyes rolled back in his head, blood streaming from his slashed wrist, Jake pressing on the cut, fat Chancey running down the cliff, David laughing/crying uncontrollably, Sue checking the boy's heartbeat.

I shook my head vigorously in an attempt to clear away these disturbing images. This was my beach. I had to make it mine again. Needed to reclaim it in some way. I began walking, crisscrossing the cove. As I paced, my gaze drifted out toward the sea. Gulls were gliding over the water, calling *skree, skree*. In the distance, a few lobsterboats dotted the horizon.

My stride slowed as I began to pay attention to the world close at hand. I'd known this comma-shaped beach all my life, but I never tired of the little discoveries to be made here. With the toe of my shoe, I overturned small stones to study their color and shape. I leaned down to pick up periwinkle shells or pieces of sea-glass that caught my eye.

The photographer in me took over and, almost automatically, I took out my Nikon 600 and fitted a 200mm lens on it. I snapped frame after frame of barnacles clinging to mussels, strands of kelp drying on pebbles, starfish and urchin stranded in tidal pools. I bracketed the shots, adjusting the F-stop, using different exposure settings. A dead plover, its wing bent awkwardly, caught my attention. With my camera, I tried to capture ringlets of water in its feathers and the blank socket that once held its eyeball.

I avoided shooting in the place where the young man had hurt himself, walking past it each time I came near the spot. But I got caught up in taking pictures, and before I knew it I was standing near the spot where we'd found him. I kept shooting, snapping snails suctioned onto pebbles, the empty shell of a horseshoe crab, a fraying piece of line that had washed ashore.

When the ring first appeared in my lens, I hardly recognized it for what it was. I was shooting directly down on a piece of driftwood when I noticed a small circular form glinting in the sand.

I knelt to pick up the object. It seemed to be a cheap gold band with a horizontal cross engraved on the front. I dropped it into the cup of my hand, bounced it around in my palm, then held it to look at the inside. There was an inscription that was too small for me to make out and then the initials *BG. B* for *Ben*?

Could the ring belong to that kid? Had he dropped it here yesterday? I didn't know his last name and I had no idea if it was his ring, but I slipped it into my pocket anyway. Twisting the 200 lens off the camera body, I packed them in the bag. Then I swung the bag over my shoulder and climbed the path up the ledges.

I used a magnifying glass to read the inscription inside the ring. *Love no other.* Maybe it's a friendship ring, I thought, as I laid the ring in my top dresser drawer, under some T-shirts.

The evening weather was mild as I walked north along Granite Road toward the Tuttle's. I wanted to check the house for Owen and Emily while their summer helper was in the hospital on the mainland. Make sure he'd left the windows shut against rain, the doors closed.

At my neighbor's house, I could see that the weathered clapboard siding was in the process of being painted white. Two stepladders supported makeshift scaffolding, and a scraper, brush, and empty paint bucket lay on the plank between them. The lawn in front of the house was only half-mowed, the mower standing in a path of cut grass. Beyond the lawn, there was a sheer drop to the sea, where water pounded against the rocks in a spray of white foam.

As I approached the house, I heard the familiar sounds of the island: surf crashing, gulls screeching, boats chugging. The back door was closed but not locked, so I pushed it open and walked into the kitchen. I went through the house quickly, closing the windows.

On my way out, something red on the kitchen table caught my eye. It was a spiral notebook. I don't really know why, just plain curiosity I guess, but I picked it up. Inside the cover were the letters *BG*. Those initials again. Ben's? Dark doodles and a cramped script covered the first page, and in some places the writer had scratched so hard with a pen that the paper was worn thin and nearly ripped through. Before I set the notebook back on the table, I read the first paragraph:

> *May 20*
>   *Happy graduation to me!!! Congratulations and all that shit. Goodbye to Bangor High. Now all my friends are getting ready to start their own lives—go to college, get jobs, get married maybe, have kids, all that regular stuff—and what am I gonna do? Probably be stuck right where I've always been, right under my old man's thumb. Nothing's ever gonna change. There's just no way to get free of that bastard. My father will go on running my life, no matter what I do.*

I slammed the cover shut. This is a personal journal, I thought as I dropped it onto the table, and none of my business.

But as I started out the door, I remembered a student in one of Grace's literature classes who had tried to commit suicide by taking an overdose of Zanax. Nobody had any clue about why she wanted to die, until her roommate found a diary that the girl had written and discovered that she'd run up enormous debts on credit cards.

I wondered if this red notebook was also a kind of death diary. Maybe there were some clues about why this boy had tried to kill himself. I don't know how long I stood in Owen and Emily Tuttle's kitchen, trying to decide whether to leave it where I'd found it or to go ahead and read the damn thing. I argued with myself back and forth. If the notebook was that boy's, he probably meant it to be private. On the other hand, if he left it there when he set out to kill himself, maybe he meant for someone to find it. Maybe he wanted someone to read it. And if I read it, maybe I'd find some answers that would help him.

Though I wasn't sure I was doing the right thing, I picked up the notebook and slipped it under my arm.

I was about to step into the tub just as Jake called. Grabbing a bath towel, I dashed into the kitchen to answer the phone.

He filled me in on the boy we'd help rescue. "They flew the kid to Knox County Airfield in Thomaston. Had an ambulance there to meet the plane. Took him over to Pen Bay Medical and right into surgery," he told me. "He's still over to the hospital. From what I understand, he's gonna pull through, sure enough. But they're keeping him in the psych ward for a few days, just the same."

"I heard the plane coming in last night," I said as I pulled the bath towel around me like a sarong. "Is Sue back on island?"

"Ayuh. When she got back from the main, guess she told Chancey all about it. He passed it on to me when I run into him over to the hardware store." I could hear Jake lighting a cigarette, then he went on, "That boy's lucky he made such a clean cut. Took a hand surgeon to get it stitched up, but his hand's gonna work good as new, from what I gather."

"How did you happen to find him anyway, Jake?"

"Pure frigging luck. I'd just got over to your place— remember me telling you David made a card for your birthday? We were bringing that over to you." The sound of Jake taking a puff on his cigarette came over the line. "Anyhow, I climbed outta the truck and happened to look down at the beach. The boy was just standing there next to the water, like he was trying to make up his mind about something. I had a feeling something weren't right, so I yelled to David to stay put and headed down."

"You were meant to be there."

Jake snorted. "Don't know about that, but I got a sneaking suspicion he might of been waiting for someone to see him. Could be wrong, though."

The water was still running in the bathroom, and it sounded as thought the tub was nearly full. "Wait a second, will you, Jake? I've got to turn the water off in the tub." When I picked up the phone again, I said, "Okay, I'm back. What did the doctors say? About the boy? Did he lose a lot of blood?"

"Guess they checked his hemo-something-or-other and found out he didn't need more blood pumped into him. According to Chancey, they're fretting more about what's going on in his noggin."

I tightened the bath towel, tucking the edge above my breasts. "What would make a kid like that want to hurt himself?"

"Beats the hell out of me."

I leaned back against the kitchen counter, cradling the phone on my shoulder. "What's his name? Did you find that out?"

"It's Ben, like you said. Last name's Gere. He's got folks in Bangor, I guess."

"I suppose the hospital called them," I said.

"Don't know," Jake replied. "No idea what the story is there." I could hear David whining in the background.

"Hang on, sis. Gotta tend to something here." I heard a soft thud as he set the phone down, then there was static on the line with Jake's and David's voices in the distance.

"Is David all right?" I asked when Jake came back on. "Is he still upset about what happened yesterday?"

"Ain't nothing wrong with him. Just wanted help getting the cover off the peanut butter jar, that's all. But last night was something else all together, you better believe. David was wicked shook up. I had a hard time getting him to settle down and go to sleep. But today he seems to have put it outta his mind, for the time being anyway."

"Well, that's a relief. What's he doing, watching television?"

"Nope. Right this minute he's making a hell of a mess fixing peanut butter crackers for himself. Before that he was sitting at the kitchen table, scribbling with his crayons. Got an inkling he's making you another birthday card. He keeps nagging to come over to see you."

"Well, bring him over tomorrow when you get in from fishing. I want to see him, too."

"We won't be out on the water long. Ain't hauling many pots until the fishing picks up."

I never said a word to him about finding the boy's red notebook. As I slipped the receiver back onto its cradle, the notebook glared at me from the counter. I touched the wire on its spine, then pushed it aside. I really was shocked at myself. How could I have done such a thing: taken someone else's property? And such an intimate item.

While soaking in the warm tub, I mulled my options. Should I take the notebook back to the Tuttle house? Should I tell someone about it? If I told anyone, it would be Sue. Should I read it first?

CHAPTER 4

Some of the notebook pages were doodled on with dark crosses, lightning bolts, lines that spiraled like tornadoes. The words were printed instead of written in cursive, and the handwriting was tiny and cramped. I settled onto the couch, tucked my feet under me, wrapped my flannel robe around my knees, and began reading:

June 3

   I'm sick & tired of dealing w/ my father. I'll never figure out what makes him tick. The only reason I took this job on the island was to get away for the summer— at least now there's some water between me and him.

   The great & mighty Pastor Ralph—Lamp of Faith Church Ministries, Bangor, Maine. Why does the fellowship buy all that crap he hands them? Why can't they see through him? But no, they think he's awesome. What a joke! They just eat it up when he says 'brothers and sisters, I'm helping you get closer to god.' Oh, sure. He's the one to do that, alright.

Maybe I didn't want to know all this about Ben. I didn't feel right about trespassing. Probably the best thing to do would be to hand the journal over to Sue and let her deal with it. She was the professional when it came to this kind of thing. But my curiosity got the best of me, and I turned the page:

LAST WON'T & TESTIMONY OF BEN GERE
(THE PRODIGAL SON)
June 4

Just can't see any way to get free of Pastor Ralph. Man, I figured once I got high school behind me, once I hit eighteen, I could move away. Far away, like to Colorado or Montana or some place & not have to put up w/ him anymore. But I don't have the dough to take off like that. My junker car sure won't get me very far.

So I came here instead. But I've only been at the Tuttle house a few days and already he's called me three times. Even out here I can't get away from him. Today I get this long boring letter—he musta put it on the damn mail plane himself. In the letter he's harping at me. Says I should come back home & work for him. Help him out w/ his church. Says I'm not smart enough to do anything else, anyway. That no one else would hire me. Says he'd be doing me a favor by letting me work for his church. Says I can live at home & save up some money for my future. Right, like he's really gonna pay me if I work for him. He says after a few years I can take off to wherever. Sure. I just don't see it happening. He'll find some way to keep me there forever. Keep me under his fucking thumb.

One thing I know, Pastor Ralph doesn't give a damn about anybody, except himself. Doesn't even have a heart.

It's like what he's got inside his fat chest is one of those cheap Valentine hearts, red velvet w/ shiny things on it. I can just see it—opens like a card & says inside SORRY, CLOSED FOR THE DAY. No wait, I bet it says DANGER, DO NOT ENTER. Hell, I don't know, probably doesn't even open. It's one of those trick cards, looks like it's supposed to open but there's no way to do it.

June 5

He called again last night. Won't leave me alone. First he says this summer's supposed to be my forty days of solitude—then he pesters me all the time. Wants to know am I siding w/ him or w/ satan? Like there's a choice.

I don't get why everybody in the fellowship puts my old man on a damn pedestal. Shit, can't they see through him? The way they act, you'd think he was god himself showing off up there in front of them, pounding the bible, shouting all that gospel stuff at them. Pastor Ralph could give god a run for his money.

Makes me sick to think of all those Sundays I sat w/ my mother in church, the good boy, sitting in one of those damn hard folding chairs—makes my ass hurt just to think of it. And it was so boring, the way he'd go on & on. I tried to think about anything else except what he was saying. But now this funny thought keeps going through my head—there was this small round window right behind him & sometimes the sunshine would come through the window & shine on him. When I was little I thought it was a halo. Can you fucking believe it?

June 7

Rules. Pastor Ralph's got rules even god couldn't think up. Like I had to read scripture every night for an hour before I went to bed. And sometimes he made my mother & me fast & pray for days on end. HE didn't have to, he said, cause he was already in god's good graces. Chosen by god, handpicked by the big man. Shit, my stomach'd be hurting & growling & there I'd be on my knees pretending to pray. Yeah, I was praying alright— for a big thick steak. Here's another rule—my mother wasn't allowed to get a job. Pastor Ralph says her only purpose is to serve him so he can serve god. And she buys that crap. One time at supper he made her lay on the floor at his feet & apologize to him because the chicken was undercooked. Shit, why'd she do that anyway, always do what he said?

June 9

Wished I was dead. There's just no getting away from him. He called again this morning. Yak. Yak. Yak. Blah blah blah. I don't even really listen to him, just say uh huh, uh huh, like I care. I don't give a damn what he has to say, not after the things he did to me.

Like the fucking cellar, man. I don't know why I was so dumb, but I never had a clue when he was gonna make me go down there. It'd just happen right out of the clear blue. He'd get tired of having me around, I guess, wanted to get rid of the kid for a while. He said it was to make me think about what living w/ satan would be like. Said it would open my heart to jesus—sure, like all I had to do was sleep on the dirt floor w/ mice & spiders & I'd be saved. That jerk. Making me stay in that fucking cellar. When I was lit-

tle I'd squeeze into a shelf w/ my mother's canned pickles & jam cause I could see the cellar window from there. That was the only light in the whole damn place.

One time my old man gets wise & blocks up the window. I'm laying there, all curled up, my eyes glued to that little bit of light, & then I see his feet. It's a Sunday cause he's still wearing his shiny black shoes from church. I can't believe this—next thing I know he's stacking wood in front of the window. Clunk, clunk, fucking clunk! Then my mother comes to the rescue. Oh sure, Sister Harriet's gonna save her little boy. What's she think she is, Batwoman or something? Shit, I can hear her out there whining & pleading w/ him. I'm thinking, don't even bother cause it won't do a damn bit of good. He keeps putting that wood in front of the window & pretty soon it gets real dark. I mean dark. Pitch black. So I shut my eyes & this stupid picture comes into my head of my old man standing in church w/ a fucking halo around him.

June 10

I'm so fucking tired. Couldn't sleep again last night. Haven't slept for days. Feel like a damn zombie. Can't deal w/ my life anymore—want it to be over. Want to just crawl in a box like my brother and not have to worry about anything anymore.

Sounds funny to say "my brother." Never even knew him—he died when he was a baby. His name was Joseph & he was just two weeks old. I remember my mother was really down after he died. Mostly, she just stayed in bed.

Something weird happened right after Joey died. My old man would go into my mother's room alot. That was bizarre right there cause it wasn't like him. Usually when she's sick, he ignores her—he's pissed she's not fixing meals or cleaning or ironing. But this time he was giving her alot of attention. I thought maybe he just wanted to see how she was doing. She was really torn up about the baby. Took it so hard, she didn't even go to the funeral. The funny part was, he wouldn't let me go into her room w/ him. Sometimes I'd try to follow, but he'd tell me to go do my chores or my homework. Then he'd close the bedroom door.

One day I got my chores done early—I think it was raking the leaves—& when I came back into the house, the bedroom door's open just a crack. I can hear my mother humming a lullaby. That one about the bough breaking. I sneak over & look in. There's my damn father w/ his mouth on her tit. Just sucking away—I think he musta been drinking her milk! She's got this blank look on her face, kind of staring up at the ceiling. But she's stroking his head & humming to him. Like he's taken the place of my baby brother.

That's why he was going into her room all the time. He didn't give a damn about the baby dying. Or about my mother. He just wanted what he fucking wanted.

Sometimes I think if he'd lived—Joseph, my brother Joey—it might have been easier on me. At least, my old man would've had someone else to rag at. He could've spread it around a little & not dumped it all on me.

June 11
Yesterday he sends me a nine page letter. Nine pages! Page after page of bible stuff. And then how much they need me at home, that my mother's really depressed since I left. If I came home it would help her alot. What a bunch

of crap. There's no way I can help my mother. If she's depressed it's because of him. Living w/ him is enough to make any sane person depressed.

Fuck him anyway.

One time he found out I'd flipped the bird at Jim Barnes. Brother Paling caught me doing it at Wednesday night bible study & told my old man. Shit, when I got home did he ever rag at me for giving the finger in church—god's holy house w/ the hard folding chairs. Seems it's blasphemous. His words, not mine. Then he goes 'It is my duty to break satan's hold on your heart.' Yeah, right. Like pretending to stick those fucking sewing needles under the fingernails of my middle fingers—both of them—was gonna do that. He was clever, though, I'll give him that. Real careful not to push the needles in deep enough to leave marks. Didn't even break the skin or make it bleed or anything. Just tormented me with the idea that he was gonna jab me.

Soon as he could see I was scared shitless, he quit. He dropped my hands—they were shaking like crazy—and slipped the needles into a piece of church stationery. Real deliberate like. Then he folded the paper & put it in his sweater pocket. The way he tapped his pocket when he walked out of the room—making damn sure I saw him do it—I knew he was saving those needles in case he ever caught me giving anyone the finger. Hey, I might be god's big mistake like he's always telling me, but I'm not stupid.

What I don't get is why my mother never stopped him. I love her, but she really is chickenshit. She'd never dare go against the old man. I can just hear him telling her, 'god wants you to do what I ask you to do & if you don't you're going against god himself.' Yeah, right. Like he's god or something.

If I have to hear one more time about the revelation he received & how he's been called to lead the people, I'll puke. Well, he's sure got those folks in his church right in his hands—could make them eat shit & believe it was honey. Like when he makes an altar call. They get really crazy. Used to scare the crap out of me when I was a kid. 'Brothers & sisters in christ, yield your hearts to the lord' he shouts & everybody just starts waving their hands in the air & yelling 'praise the lord' & ol' Pastor Ralph answers 'thank jesus.' Sometimes he gets so worked up, he's actually got fucking tears rolling down his cheeks.

June 13

My old man has to make sure I don't get big in the head. Like it's his personal mission, cutting me down to size. So he calls this morning & bitches at me, says why can't I make up my mind & just come back home & help him out w/ the church. Says I'll never amount to any-thing else, might as well be working for him. Like that's what I really want to do.

He's always fucking me over, one way or another. I remember this one time I was bragging at the supper table about how I'd sold the most candy bars for our church fund raiser. And he says 'Son,' he says, 'you are guilty of fleshly, human pride. I will pray over you & cast out the demon.' Then he goes, 'It's clear you need spiritual authority. You must submit to god's discipline.' And, of course, god speaks directly to him so god musta told him about the marbles. Cause I got to kneel on the floor w/ marbles under my knees & if I let one slip out, he puts 2 back in its place. For a whole hour it seemed, leaning on those fucking marbles. Last count—4 marbles under my right knee, 3 under the left. And then when he hears my mother coming, that's when he says I can stand up. Yeah, right. He doesn't want her to know what he's been doing to me. As if she'd do anything about it. But, jesus, I can't get up. Can't get my fucking legs to work right.

June 14

I used to piss the bed. For years my mother covered for me so my old man wouldn't find out. She always kept a piece of plastic over my mattress & washed my sheets every day. When my father did find out he was raving mad—like I was doing it on purpose or something. He yells, 'If you were right w/ god you would have control of your bodily functions.'

By the time I turned eleven I was doing really good, but then one night I slipped up. I remember there'd been a revival meeting that Friday & I got home late & I was really tired when I went to bed. Saturday morning, I get this really rude awakening. My father's standing next to my bed, yelling at me 'You've soiled your bed. I can smell the stench. Get up & get showered.' Then he makes my mother hang the sheet out on the line, but of course he won't let her wash it first. And there's this big yellow stain in the middle of it & all the neighbors see it & it stays there that whole day.

And then that night I had a terrible dream. I dreamt my father made me wear that pissy sheet to church! Over my shoulders, like a fucking robe. A stinking yellow robe. Made me sit in the front row w/ my mother & he announced to the whole damn fellowship 'There sits a boy who is unclean.' He was pointing his bible at me. 'An unclean boy in the house of jesus! What should we do about it, brethren?'

The dream seemed like it was real. Like I was sitting in the front row, sinking way down in my chair. I could feel my face burning & I wanted to fucking die right there. Everyone was staring at me & I musta stunk cause nobody would sit close to me. 'Brothers & sisters,' my father yelled, 'help me appeal to jesus to help this sinful boy.' And they all shouted, 'lord, help him!' My mother was praying too. I could see her lips moving but she was looking at the floor & I couldn't hear what she was saying.

I woke up in a cold sweat, thinking I must be evil, just like my father always says, if the whole church has to pray for me. Then I remembered, it was just a dream.

June 15—2:30 am

I can't go on w/ this pain anymore, just want it all behind me. I want to go to sleep & have it all be over & be free of him forever. Every newspaper I get hold of, I read the obituaries & imagine how my old man will feel reading my obit. I hope when I'm dead & he's looking down at me in the casket, he remembers all the things he did to me.

My father's weird. All my life he's acted like he's mad I was ever born. I'm used to him being mean to me. Shit, I even expect it. But one time he did something I still haven't figured out.

I was about 13 when it happened. That night I get home from the library around 9:00. My old man's being pretty nice when I come in, which is a surprise right there. Just to be safe, I keep my distance from him & hurry & run upstairs & brush my teeth. Then I quick get out of my clothes & jump into bed. I pull up the quilt & turn off the light & I'm just starting to doze off when he comes into my room! I remember feeling really scared

*cause he's never done that before. I quick close my eyes &
pretend I'm already asleep.*

*I hear him go over to the window, so I open my eyes
a little & watch to see what's he's up to. He's just standing there, staring out at the moon or something. Like he's
praying. Then, out of nowhere, he starts crying. I swear
to god, he's crying. He's not making a huge noise or anything, but he's kinda hunched over & he's got his hands
over his eyes. His back's to me, but it looks like he's wiping his eyes. Seems like forever he's over there crying.
Weird, man. So fucking weird.*

*Next thing I know, he's standing right next to my
bed. I make believe I'm sleeping, but I'm scared I'm gonna
breathe loud or cough or something. Then the damnedest
thing. And I still don't get this. He leans down & kisses
me on the forehead. Shit. In my whole life, that's the only
time my father's ever kissed me.*

June 16

*Maybe my old man's right—maybe I am full of sin.
Not good for anything. I'm tired of thinking about it.
Tired of hearing his voice in my head. So fucking fucking
tired.*

*If I was dead & in the ground I wouldn't have to think
about any of this anymore. This picture keeps popping into
my mind—I'm laying in a casket up front in his church,
wearing my new graduation suit, arms folded over my
chest & it's like I'm sleeping. Everybody's there, all the
church folk & relatives—my mother's crying. Nobody can
understand why I did it & everybody's feeling sorry for me.
I like this part best—my old man's really nervous & the fellowship hasn't ever seen him like that before. I can just pic-*

ture it. He's staring down at me in this coffin & he tries to act like he's sad but inside he's pissed cause I've embarrassed him. The great preacher—Pastor Ralph—able to save all souls. Except his own son's.

June 17

His phone bill's gonna be outrageous. Good, I hope he shits when he gets it. Then maybe he'll stop calling me so much. Gets so I hate to hear the phone ring. I thought of not answering it or taking it off the hook. But it might be the Tuttles or something to do w/ their house, so I gotta answer.

I was just watching a couple of squirrels chasing each other in the tree outside & it got me thinking about a squirrel I killed once. I'd made a sling shot from a forked twig & a piece of bicycle inner tube. Kept it hidden in my room between the mattress & the box spring. Sometimes when my old man wasn't around—like when he was at the church or something—I'd take it out & practice target shooting in the back yard. Got so I could knock over a tin can from fifty feet.

Anyway, I killed a squirrel. It was just sitting there real still near the stone fence & I wanted to see if I could hit it. Man! My rock caught it right behind the ear . . . the thing fell right over w/ its paws sticking straight up in the air. So I go over & nudge it w/ my sneaker, & you know what? It fucking jerked. Like it was having some damn death spasm or something.

I wonder if that's what happens when a person dies? Does it hurt and make your muscles jerk, or do you just kind of go into something like a coma? I hope you just become unconscious, don't feel a thing. I wouldn't want it to hurt.

Anyway, I quick covered the dead squirrel w/ some leaves so my father wouldn't see. Shit, how was I supposed to know he'd snuck up behind me? All of a sudden I feel his hand on my shoulders—damn near jump out of my skin! 'Now what evil thing have you done?' he says. I tried to explain that I'd never killed anything before. Swore I never would again.

But that wasn't good enough for him. He yells, 'Hand that over to me!' & yanks the damn slingshot right out of my back pocket. Next thing I know he's down on his knees. What's he gonna do, pray for that stupid squirrel? I'm wondering. But no. He digs around in the grass & all the leaves until he finds the rock I'd used. It had some blood on it & a gross hunk of fur. 'These will stay in plain view, where they'll remind you of your sin,' he preaches at me.

Next thing I know, my sling shot & that little bloody rock are locked up in the glass cabinet in the living room. Right where I'm gonna see them every damn day. On a shelf next to a picture of jesus. That one where he's pulling his shirt open & there's this huge red heart that looks like it's gonna fall out of his chest.

Hope I can sleep tonight. I work hard enough during the day—scraping this house to get it ready to paint. You'd think I'd sleep like a log. But I haven't slept decent in weeks.

June 18—3:40 am
Got another letter from my old man today. Wants to know how my forty days in the wilderness are coming along. And he's still harping at the same old thing— wants to know if I'm gonna come back & help him w/ his

church. Yeah, right. That's the last thing in the world I want to do. But what else can I do?

I don't want to ever see Pastor Ralph again. Ever! Don't want to deal w/ him at all.

My mind keeps racing. Been thinking about the Sunday when the evangelist from N. C. came to town. My old man was all excited because this guy was famous or something & he was bringing his 10-year-old kid along & they were going to be guest preachers at our church. I musta been about fifteen & one morning my old man meets me at the top of the stairs. You could knock me over w/ a feather cause he's real friendly to me & even gives me a big smile. He says, 'Hurry up, son. Get ready to serve your lord.' And he seems so nice I quick slick down my hair & put on a pair of chino pants, blue button-down oxford, navy blazer, red tie & I even shine my loafers w/ the edge of my bedspread. And when I run downstairs my old man's still smiling & he's actually holding the front door open for me.

We get into the car & he tells me to sit in the front seat & makes my mother sit in back. I like the way he's treating me but I'm afraid I'll blow it so I try to act really cool. For a minute there, I'm even thinking maybe all the bad stuff's over & from now on things'll be different. Maybe everything's going to be alright. I'm even remembering the time he came into my room & kissed me, & I'm thinking maybe it means something after all. When we get to church my old man puts me up front w/ him & this famous evangelist & his kid. And I sit there the whole time they're preaching the gospel.

Of course, it doesn't last—him being nice. The next day, after that evangelist & his boy head back to N. C. where they came from, things go back to normal. My old

*man's smile disappears & he's grouchy again, even more
of a bastard than before. Go figure—how come he picked
that one day to like me & hated me all the others?*

June 19 (the end)
 *Haven't slept in weeks. Feel like crap. Wished I was
dead.*
 *Almost every night I've been going over to a little
cemetery I found that has really old headstones. They're
like covered with moss and half tipping over. You can't
hardly read the writing on them but the dates are like in
the 1800's and some of them say 'lost at sea' which I think
is cool. Sometimes I go there and just lay on the grass
near one of those.*
 *Last night I took this damn ring over to the cemetery
& buried it next to one of the gravestones, but then when
I got ready to leave I dug it up & put it back in my pocket. I've had the ring all summer, but I've never worn it.
Not once. And I fucking never will. My old man gave it
to me on graduation day. Isn't that weird? As I see it, it's
his cute little way of telling me nothing's ever going to
change. I'm like a bull w/ a ring through my nose—and
he's got hold of the other end of the rope. Just jerking me
around.*
 *But something is gonna change!!! I'm fed up w/
everything, tired of my life, so damn tired of dealing w/
him. I'm gonna push him off that fucking pedestal the fellowship has him on. How will the mighty Pastor Ralph
ever explain about his only begotten son?*

CHAPTER 5

I stayed up all night absorbed in Ben's journal. I'd read a few pages, get disgusted, throw it down. Then I'd slug down some coffee while I paced the floor, brooding over what I'd read. After a while, I'd pick it up again and tackle some more pages. The sun was coming up by the time I flung the notebook onto the couch for the final time. What a miserable childhood Ben had suffered! What an appalling father!

I took my cup out to the kitchen and tossed the dregs of my cold coffee down the sink—it was my fourth cup. I was wired, though my body ached with exhaustion. I had to get moving, or I would collapse.

The lawn mower wouldn't start. I yanked the starter rope until my arm hurt. When it still wouldn't catch, I drained the old gas and added a new mixture of gas and oil. Then I sanded the spark plug and replaced it. Finally, the thing sputtered and took hold. I mowed the lawn almost at full tilt, pushing it fast and furiously, chewing up the patchy grass. Sweat dripped off my forehead by the time I finished.

A long shower cooled off my body, but it didn't wash off the loathing I felt for Ben's father. I needed to talk with someone about the revelations in the notebook. Carrying it under my arm, I jumped into my Escort and headed toward the village.

Sue had finished with her morning patients and was glad to take a break. "What's wrong with you?" she asked, pushing aside some reports on her desk. "You look like you're ready to fight a war."

"I'm mad enough to take on the whole damn world!" I dropped into a chair in her office. "I found something that belongs to that boy who tried to kill himself. Here." I shoved the notebook across her desk.

"What this?" Sue drummed her fingers on the cover.

"Open it."

She flipped it open and read the first page. "Interesting." She swiveled around in her chair and lifted a coffeepot from the credenza. "Want some?" she asked over her shoulder.

"No. I've had enough to last me all week." Fat Alice, sassy as ever, sauntered into the room and settled herself on my feet.

Sue swung back around and set her steaming cup on the desk. "So, tell me about this notebook."

While she drank her coffee, I told her what the diary revealed about Ben's father.

"No wonder the kid's a wreck," Sue said. "That helps explain why he would attempt suicide. Have you told anyone else?"

"No. I feel guilty as hell for having taken it and read it."

"You did the right thing. Gives me some clues about the best way to treat him when he gets back to the island." Sue pulled a few dead leaves from an African violet on her desk and dropped them into the wastebasket.

With my thumb and index finger I snipped off a limp, brown leaf facing my side of the desk and tossed it into the wastebasket. "Is he coming back?"

"As far as I know." Sue stood and picked up a pitcher of water and ice cubes from the credenza. Leaning over and being careful not to drop any of the ice, she poured a few drops of water onto the violet. "I had a telephone conference with Dr. Turner this morning. The Gere boy's not talking much, and he refuses to let the hospital notify his parents."

"I'll take a little of that," I said, pointing to the pitcher. Then I asked, "Can he do that? Not tell his parents?"

"He's eighteen." Sue poured a paper cup with water and handed it to me. "It's his choice."

The cold water felt good going down my throat. "How much longer will they keep him at Pen Bay?"

Sue set the pitcher on the credenza and eased back into her desk chair. "He might show up tomorrow, *if* he's coming here. We can't hold him in the psych ward for longer than seventy-two hours."

"I should get that notebook back to the Tuttle house before then. Do you think I should tell anyone else about it—Chancey maybe?" Fat Alice was plopped heavily across the toes of my shoes, purring.

"Not just yet," Sue said. "Let's see how the Gere boy is doing first. In fact, leave the notebook here with me. I want to read it through."

"You'll find it interesting," I said. "The way he writes is drastically different from the way he seems in person. The few times I saw him last summer, I got the impression that he was timid. But in his journal he comes across as a very angry young man. I mean really pissed. Mostly at his father."

"Most likely, he represses that rage and turns it

inward—to the point of wanting to kill himself." Sue set the notebook on the desk.

"Oh, let me tell you what else I found." I told her about the ring.

"So you think the Gere boy dropped it on the beach the day of his suicide attempt?"

I nodded, nudging Fat Alice because she was chewing on the laces of my shoes. She heaved herself off my feet and lumbered over to the carpet, where she stretched luxuriously in a patch of sun.

"Let me get this straight," Sue said. "You found the ring in the sand? And it had what inside?"

"The initials *BG*. And then it said *love no other*."

"Must have been from a girlfriend, don't you think?"

"That would make sense, wouldn't it? But nothing seems to be making much sense lately," I said, crimping my paper cup and dumping it into the wastebasket. "The ring was from his father. A graduation gift, I guess. Ben writes about it in the journal." I handed her the red notebook.

Fat Alice whined as she followed us out of Sue's office; she wasn't happy that I'd dislodged her from my feet. In the waiting room, a young mother was reading a copy of *Redbook*. A toddler stood near her knee, stroking the mother's dress and sucking his thumb, his nose runny. He smiled at the cat. A little girl with brown pigtails, who reminded me of myself when I was in first grade, was sitting at a small table building legos. A wad of cotton was stuffed in her ear, and she was coughing.

Sue waved to them, then whispered to me, "I haven't forgotten your birthday. We'll get together soon and celebrate, okay? I have something for you."

I nodded, and Sue turned to her patients. With a smile, she leaned over and scooped up the baby. "What a big boy you're getting to be, Jimmy Halstead. And look at you, Jenny," she said to the little girl, tweaking her pigtail. "What are you building there?" As I left, Sue had the baby on her hip and was leading them into her office, listening intently as the mother told her how the kids had summer colds and at first she wasn't worried, but now it had been weeks and they couldn't seem to shake them. I saw Sue pat the mother's arm, then rub the top of the little girl's head.

On the drive home, I realized I felt much better just for having talked with Sue. It occurred to me that I always felt better after being with her.

Jake and David turned into my driveway right behind me. As they got out of the truck, I asked, "Have you had lunch?"

"Nope," Jake said. "But don't go to any bother."

"I haven't eaten either. You can help me put together some sandwiches," I said, leading them into the cottage. David plopped down on the porch daybed while Jake and I went into the kitchen. As I got out the bread and bologna, I asked, "Have you heard anything more about that boy?"

"It's an odd tale, that one," Jake said, reaching into the refrigerator. "Ain't got one iota why he cut himself. Chancey asked me what I knew about his background. Hell, I said, I ain't seen him around the island but a few times. Don't know a thing about him 'cept he's been living over to Owen Tuttle's, painting the place."

I lined up three slices of bread on the counter, and Jake spread mustard on them. He asked, "You talked with Sue at all since this happened?"

I slapped bologna onto the bread he'd fixed, two slices of meat each for Jake and David, one for me. "Just came back from there," I said. "She doesn't know much either.

Just that Ben's going to be okay—and he's most likely coming back to the island."

David walked through the kitchen on his way to the bathroom. "Lunch will be ready soon," I called after him.

"Okay, Marfa," he said as he disappeared down the hallway.

Jake spread the Hellman's thickly on more slices of bread and squeezed the sandwiches together. He and I had eaten bologna sandwiches this way, with a thick mixture of mustard and mayonnaise, all our lives. "Do you know anything about that boy, Martha? With him living close by and all?"

I decided not to tell Jake about the notebook, at least not until Sue had read it. As I put together a plate of carrot sticks and celery, I avoided looking at him. "Grace and I met Ben a few times last summer, when we were visiting Emily. But, really, I hardly know him. I haven't run into him since I got here this summer, and he was on the island for such a short time last year. I always thought he seemed shy. The type who keeps pretty much to himself."

Just then, David clumped into the kitchen, smiling broadly. "Marfa, look." He held out his left hand. A gold chain gleamed in his palm. "I keep?"

"What'cha got there, pal?" Jake asked as he reached for David's hand. "What's this?"

"Oh, God, that's Grace's necklace!" I gasped. "Give it here, David."

David pulled back. "I keep," he insisted, thrusting his hands under his armpits.

Jake's face blanched. "Where'd he get Gracie's necklace?"

"On my dresser," I said. "David, you know better than to take things from my room. Now, give it to Aunt Martha."

"No!" He shook his head, his feet spread wide and planted squarely on the floor. "Mine!"

Trying to soothe him with the softness of my voice, I purred, "Just let auntie take a look at it." David could be very stubborn; he didn't budge. I needed to get that necklace from him. I tried another tactic. "You know, we're about ready to eat. I'm really hungry. How about you, David?"

He kept his hands tightly clasped under his armpits, but he relaxed his shoulders. "David, help set the table," I said. "You can use those small plates on that bottom shelf." I placed my hand on his shoulder and steered him toward the cupboard. "We need three plates, and three paper napkins."

David let his hands fall, but jammed the one holding the gold chain into his pants pocket. Awkwardly, he set the table with his free hand.

Throughout lunch, David kept his left hand, the one holding the chain, clenched in his lap. He was left-handed, so he made a mess trying to eat with his right hand, getting mustard and mayonnaise all over his face and on the tip of his nose.

"When's the lobster fishing expected to pick up?" I asked Jake, hoping to distract David.

Jake ignored my question and muttered under his breath, "I don't know why David's so damn bent on having that necklace." Jake pushed his plate away, his sandwich untouched, and lifted a pack of Marlboros from his pocket. He sat tapping the package on the table, deep in thought, studying his son.

I watched David closely too. My only goal was to get Grace's chain from him. To do that, I had to divert attention away from it. "When's the fishing going to get better?" I asked my brother again.

Jake put a Marlboro in his mouth but didn't light it. "It's always slow this time of year," he said, the cigarette dangling on his lip.

I filled his cup with two rounded tablespoons of instant Maxwell and hot water, then dumped in three heaping spoonfuls of sugar—Jake liked his coffee black and sweet. Feigning more interest in his fishing, I inquired, "*The Sybil* running okay?"

"Had her in dry dock until a month ago." Jake removed the unlit cigarette that was hanging from his mouth. His cup was steaming, and he waved his hand over it to cool it. After a few sips of coffee, he seemed to relax and began to talk about the repairs he'd made to his boat. "Took a good part of the winter to overhaul my gear. Had to tinker some with the engine. The bilge pump needed replacing. There's always something that's crying to be fixed."

I half-listened as he explained about the repairs he'd made. Out of the corner of my eye I watched David, but he clutched the necklace tightly.

"On top of that," Jake went on, "I had to do all the regular stuff—scrape off the old paint and sand her smooth, caulk the seams. Jesus, it's getting to be a bitch to paint that hull every year. Near cut my thumb off with the damn scraper. Had to have Sue give me a tetanus shot and stitch it up."

David dropped the chewed crust of his sandwich onto his plate. "Man blood," he cried. "Bad."

"You mean Papa?" I asked. "That was months ago."

"No! Yes'day." David began twisting a strand of his hair. I realized he must be thinking of the Gere boy.

"I scared. Red blood." David jumped up from his chair.

What a relief to hear the clink of Grace's gold chain as it landed on the floor. Quickly, I stood up and circled my arms around David. "That guy on the beach is going to be all right. You don't have to worry about him."

David was trembling. "Him no die?"

"No. He'll be okay. You'll probably see him again some-time this summer," I said as I led David out to the porch. Jake followed us, then stepped outside for a smoke.

Gently, I pushed David into the wicker rocker and pat-ted his arm. "You sit here and watch the ocean while I get us some dessert. You like Oreo cookies, don't you?"

David's eyes lit up. "Black ones?"

"Yes, and wonderful white cream in the middle. Do you want a glass of milk to dip the cookies in?" I left David nodding his head and rocking the chair so vigorously it inched across the green plank porch floor.

As soon as I stepped into the kitchen, I got down on my knees and searched under the table for Grace's gold chain. I found a carrot stick that David had dropped, and a crust of bread. The chain was wedged next to the one chair that had been empty. I picked it up and held it close to my heart, taking a deep sigh. But my heart didn't slow its heavy beat-ing until the gold chain was back in my bedroom, draped over the rosewood box on the dresser.

David's eyes lit up when I carried the cookies and milk out to the porch. He dug right into them. First he split each Oreo, sliding the two halves from each other and greedily licking the filling. When he had a pile of chocolate wafers, he ate them one by one, dunking each into milk before he moved it messily to his mouth. His white T-shirt became spattered with chocolate and took on the appearance of a Rorschach inkblot.

Jake paced the lawn in front of the porch steps, smoking one cigarette after another. He seemed in a hurry to leave, but I had no idea what had upset him. "Ain't you done yet, David? Jesus, how long's it take to eat a few cookies?" he called through the screen.

"He's almost ready," I said as I handed David a wet

washcloth to wipe his face. I tried to wipe off his shirt, but it was hopeless. I just managed to spread the chocolate around into one dark stain. But David was happy; he'd enjoyed his cookies and his belly was full.

When they left, I went into my bedroom again to check that the gold chain was still there. It was. Even though it was still the middle of the afternoon, bed never looked so good. Completely worn out, I crawled into it and slept the sleep of the dead.

It shouldn't have been a surprise to me when Sue showed up that evening carrying a Mylar balloon and a package the size of a shirt box wrapped with a huge lavender bow. I was lying in the hammock, reading a new text on teaching theory. She laid the package in my lap and tied the balloon to the webbing of the hammock, then nudged my arm to set me swaying. The balloon bobbed above me, purple with yellow lettering that read *Fifty is just the beginning*.

"What's all this?" I laughed.

"I told you I had something for your birthday. And that's not all," she said, tempting me by waving a small gold-foil box in front of my nose. "I come bearing Godiva chocolates."

"Well, that's worth getting out of this hammock for."

"No need. Now that you're a half-century, you'll want all the rest you can get." She poked my ribs. "Just lie there and nibble while I build us a fire." I couldn't resist. I peeled back the gold cover and bit into dark cream as she gathered driftwood from a pile I'd made behind the Adirondack chairs. In the fire pit, she layered pinecones and dry needles for kindling, then mounded the driftwood like a tee-pee, the smallest sticks at the bottom. The fire was blazing when I forced myself out of the hammock and went over to join her.

I sank into the chair beside her and waved the gift with the lavender bow. "Do I open this?"

Sue took a candy from the gold box I'd placed on the arm of her chair.

Her words were garbled with chocolate when she said, "Or you can just admire the wrapping."

Dusk was coming on, shadows settling on the lawn, the sea below shushing in the cove. A driftwood log shifted in the fire while flames leapt and danced, the smell of burning pine drifting into the night air. I untied the ribbon and playfully looped it around Sue's neck, then lifted the cover off the box. Whatever was inside was wrapped in purple tissue paper that was flecked with gold stars. I pulled back the tissue and found a jersey sleep shirt. Purple, of course. Shaking out the folds, I held it up and read out loud what it said on the front: *This Is What 50 Looks Like.* "God save us then," I said, laughing and slipping it over my sweater.

I spent most of the next day making repairs around the cottage. The hinges on the screen door of the porch had rusted badly over the winter. The last time I was at the hardware store, I'd bought new ones. Removing the screws with a Phillips, I took the door off and replaced the hinges. Then I re-hung the door, moving it back and forth, testing the swing. That was much better; now there wouldn't be that annoying squeak every time someone opened the door.

By placing bricks under them, I leveled the porch steps, which had settled and listed badly. I noticed a rotting tread and made a mental note to buy a new piece of lumber for it during my next trip to the village.

I was snipping peony blossoms for a bouquet late in the afternoon when the sheriff's jeep drove by. The Gere boy was sitting in the passenger seat. I waved and Chancey raised his hand, but the boy sat stiffly staring out the windshield.

At suppertime, I tossed together a cold salad of pasta, tuna, and mayo, arranged it on a bed of lettuce, added two sourdough biscuits, and sealed it all in a Tupperware dish. On the walk to the Tuttle house, mosquitoes and black flies pestered me so I hurried along Granite Road, swatting at them with my free hand.

Before I had a chance to knock, the door swung open. A young man stood with his hand on the inside knob. He wore a faded blue polo shirt, worn but clean jeans, and Reeboks. There was a mole just above one eyebrow. His blond hair, though long enough to fall against his collar, was combed neatly.

"Hi," I said. "I'm Martha Felkins, from next door. You can't see my house from here, but it's the next cottage down the road." I motioned in that direction with my head.

"H-h-hello," he stammered, a flush creeping up his neck to his cheekbones. He seemed bashful—not at all like the angry young man in his journal.

Brushing past him into the kitchen, I explained, "I brought along some supper. Thought you might not have much here to eat after being gone for a few days." As I set the Tupperware container on the counter, I started chatting nervously. "This old kitchen is so familiar to me. I used to come here a lot when I was a kid—Owen Tuttle and I were in the same class at the island school. When Owen married Emily and brought her over from the mainland, we became friends too. I can still see Emily standing right there at that counter rolling out cookie dough. Have you ever tasted her gingerbread cookies? Or her date-filled?" I patted the top of the Tupperware dish. "You'll want to put this in the refrigerator if you don't eat it right away."

I turned back toward him. He still stood at the door, his hand on the knob, and he appeared dazed. "Gosh, excuse me," I said. "I just rushed right in here. You might not even remember me. We met a couple of times last summer when you were staying here with Owen and Emily. And you probably don't remember, but I was on the beach the day you got hurt. My brother Jake was there, too. And his son, David. You're Ben, right?"

His eyes did not meet mine, they flitted away nervously. "Ben Gere," he said, practically swallowing the words.

Suddenly I felt tired and unsure if I should have come. "Do you mind if I sit down?"

Ben Gere blushed. "Have a chair." Moving across the room, he pulled out a yellow-padded chrome chair using his good hand. A gauze bandage covered the wrist of his other hand.

"Does it hurt?" I pointed to his wrist as I took the seat he offered.

Again he avoided my eyes. "A little."

"Did they give you something for it?"

"Pain pills while I was in the hospital. Tylenol with codeine, or something like that. But Doctor Turner wouldn't let me bring any home. They made me feel kind of woozy, anyway." He pulled out another chair and sat down, awkwardly resting his injured arm on the table. His Adam's apple moved up and down as he kept clearing his throat.

I had an urge to touch his shoulder. Instead, I said, "I should go. Let you eat your supper and rest."

But as I started to stand up, he stopped me. "Maybe you could stay a little while?"

I sat back down. "Sure."

"You don't need to," he stammered. "I mean if you've got something else you want to do."

"I can stay as long as you like," I said, setting my elbows on the table. "I've been working all day in my flower gardens. Feels good just to be sitting." I attempted a little laugh, but it sounded awkward.

"Doesn't need to be for very long," he said, his eyes on the table. "It's just that . . . I mean . . . well, I got used to people being around when I was in the hospital."

For a moment, I studied him. He seemed so exposed, so raw. I'd had students like that—ones who seemed oddly innocent in an awkward kind of way, like they weren't quite grown up enough to face the brutality of the world. I always felt protective toward those kinds of students, even though I knew there was no way of shielding them from harsh reality, and that it was not good to shield them. "Do you think you were you ready to come back?" I asked gently.

He shrugged, never lifting his eyes from the table.

"Look, Ben, let me fix this supper for you. While you're eating, I'll wash up those few dishes in the sink and straighten up a bit."

He sat listlessly, so I went ahead and set the table and dished up the salad. I ate too, watching him as he cleaned his plate and had seconds.

He cleared the table, and I washed up the supper dishes and the few that'd been sitting in the sink the three days he was gone. As I hung the dishtowel over the edge of the sink, I said. "Why don't you come back to my place for the night?"

"Oh, I don't think so," he said, a flush returning to his neck.

"Why not? I've got plenty of room. Do you remember Grace—she was here with me last summer? Well," I turned away as I said this, "she died last fall. Maybe you hadn't heard. I think her accident happened after you'd left the island."

Ben didn't say anything.

I picked up my Tupperware container from the dish drainer and turned back to face him. "Well, anyway, I'm alone there now. It'd be nice to have company. It'd be like you were doing me a favor." I think he bought this last lie, because he nodded his head, though he still didn't look at me.

By the time Ben Gere and I reached my cottage, the moon was visible even though daylight hadn't completely left the sky. As he climbed the porch steps, he nearly stumbled. He held his left arm close to his body, which probably threw off his balance.

"I need to replace that middle step," I said as I followed behind him. "It sags a little." Pulling the screen door shut and latching it, I said, "Why don't you take a breather there on the daybed while I put fresh sheets on the bed in David's room."

"Are you sure I'm not in the way?"

"Of course not. Sit down now and rest. I'll get your bed ready."

When he sat down on the daybed, the springs buckled and squeaked. Tiredly, he slipped off his green nylon windbreaker and slumped against the wall.

I left him there while I made up the single bed in the small room off the kitchen. Then I stepped back onto the sun porch to ask, "Would you like a glass of milk or something?"

His face took on a grim look, and his reply was surprisingly harsh. "I don't drink milk."

Taken aback by the hard way he said this, I offered, "Oh. Well then, how about gin?" He looked at me blankly, so I added, "Just joking. Lemonade okay?"

He swung his eyes to the floor and mumbled, "Sure."

I brought out two glasses of lemonade. He drank his in one gulp.

"Would you like to turn in and call it a night?" I asked.

"I'd kind of like to just sit here a while."

I didn't know if he wanted to be alone or if he wanted me nearby. I sat down in the wicker rocker. With night coming on, the air had turned chilly, and I smoothed an afghan over my lap. "Looks as if it's going to be a bright moon," I said. We sat for a while in uncomfortable silence. "Nine o'clock already, and it's just now getting dark. I like these long days, don't you, Ben? It's about the time of the summer solstice, isn't it? I remember one year on the solstice I got this crazy idea that Grace and Sue and I should have a ceremony of some sort. I must have been reading some feminist book. Anyway, for some reason, a ritual of some sort seemed like a good idea to me. So, you won't believe this, I convinced them to go down to the beach with me at midnight and light candles. Grace went along with it, but she thought it was downright silly." I laughed at the memory of her complaining about hiking down the path at night with a bunch of candles and matches, that it was just hocus pocus, ridiculous magic. I took a sip of lemonade, then wiped the condensation from the bottom of the glass before I set it back down on the wicker stand. "Grace taught at B.U., did you know that?"

He was sitting with his head resting against the wall, and he had a blank look, as if he had no idea what I was talking about.

"You know, Boston University? Grace was on the English faculty. Her interest was in modern American short story." I rattled on as Ben continued to stare at me blankly. "I'm in the art department at the Boston Institute of Art. That's at Lesley College. My medium is photography, mostly black-and-white." *Shut up, Martha,* I thought to myself, *you sound as if you're filling out a job application.*

"Cool," he mumbled, but I was sure he could care less.

When Ben didn't make any further attempt at conversation, I finished my lemonade and stood up. "In the morning I'm going berrying. There usually are wild strawberries over by Lincoln Quarry. Want to come along?"

He glanced down at his bandaged wrist and shrugged his shoulders.

"You won't have to do anything. We'll bring a blanket for you to sit on. Being out in the sun will be good for you."

"Well, maybe."

I stood up and folded the afghan over the back of the rocker. "I'm going to bed so I'll be ready bright and early."

He walked over to the green gingerbread railing and stood looking through the screen. "I'll stay here on the porch for a while if it's okay."

"Of course. When you're ready, you can sleep in that bedroom that's just off the kitchen. The bathroom's right next door to it, and I set out some fresh towels for you. Just come in whenever you want to."

"Thanks," he muttered, placing the palm of his injured hand on the screen. "It's a really bright moon."

"Beautiful, isn't it? The way it reflects on the water."

He didn't answer, just stood looking out at the night. I wondered if he might be thinking of the cove below, of what he'd done to himself on that beach just a few days ago. "Well, good night, Ben," I said, as I crossed the threshold into the cottage, headed toward my own room. I left the kitchen light on for him.

CHAPTER 6

In the morning while the Gere boy was still sleeping, I called Sue and let her know he was with me. "I don't think he's ready to be alone," I told her.

"Well, don't take on too much," she said. "Bring him over to the clinic in the next day or so. I want to check that wrist. And maybe I can get him to talk."

Ben got up not long after and seemed a little more at ease with me than he had the night before. At breakfast, he didn't say much, and he refused milk for his cereal, just ate it dry. But he washed up the bowls and cups while I put away the Cheerios and emptied coffee grounds from the pot. I noticed too that he'd left his room neat, having smoothed the navy bedspread and opened the window shade.

When we got to Lincoln Quarry, I pulled into a field behind the quarry and parked. "It's early in the season for strawberries, but I think we can find a few," I said, stepping out of the car. "Grace and I used to pick berries in this field. We liked to make strawberry jam." I spread a plaid blanket and motioned for him to sit down.

He hesitated. "I shouldn't just sit here while you work."

"Picking berries isn't work," I said. "It's more like meditation."

Reluctantly, he dropped onto the blanket in a cross-legged position. Grabbing the wire handle of a quart pail, I told him, "I'll start over there—some of those plants look ripe."

I pulled a wide-brimmed hat onto my head and walked over to the patch of wild berries. Sitting on the grass, I began picking the few dusty red berries that were scattered among the mostly green ones. I enjoyed sitting in the sun, listening to a cardinal calling from high in a maple tree, and taking my time with the picking. After about an hour, I'd managed to find enough ripe strawberries to half-fill the pail.

As I stood up, I shook the kinks out of my legs and rubbed the ache in the small of my back. I swatted at a yellow jacket as I reached down to pick up the pail, knocking the pail over and spilling berries onto the ground. "Damn," I said.

Ben came up behind me. "The bees have been bothering me too."

"Look at the mess I've made." I knelt and began picking up the berries one by on, plopping them into the pail. He squatted beside me to help, using his uninjured hand to pick up spilled berries.

"I should have just ignored the damn thing," I said. "But a bee stung Grace one time on the bottom lip, and ever since then they make me nervous." I glanced around the ground. The strawberries had been small and pitiful to begin with, and it was disheartening to see them scattered on the grass, some crushed by our feet. I shrugged and continued collecting as many as I could. "When she was stung, her lip became all red and swollen, and then I panicked that her tongue and throat would swell up too. I was afraid her breathing might get choked off, you know?"

"Was she allergic to bees?" Ben asked as he brushed a piece of grass from a berry.

"Turns out she was. She didn't know it, though. I remember she kept saying the swelling would go down, that I shouldn't worry. But her mouth sounded full of cotton, and that didn't seem right to me. I was scared and insisted she get into the car, then I drove like hell over to the clinic. Sue gave her a shot of adrenaline, and after that the swelling went down."

After we'd scooped up all the berries, we walked back to where we'd left the blanket. We picked it up and folded it, I on one end and Ben on the other. When we brought our edges together, he kept his eyes down and quickly stepped back after I'd taken the blanket from him. I draped it over my arm, and he carried the pail back to the car. As we climbed into the Escort and I switched on the ignition, I said, "I'll need to clean these berries really well. They're all full of grass and stuff."

"I can help," he said shyly, staring out the side window as we drove away from the quarry.

After we washed and hulled the berries, and set them on a shelf in the refrigerator, I asked Ben to help me patch a hole in the door to the screen porch. Handing him the wire cutters, I asked, "Can you handle these?"

"I think so." He took them with his good hand.

"Cut out a square that's smaller than this," I said holding up the new piece of screening. "Cut around that little hole where the screen's broken through. Just even out the edges."

Slowly and carefully, he snipped a hole in the screen door. I could have done it faster myself. "Good. Now I can sew this new piece over that."

He stood at the bottom of the steps and watched as I worked the needle in and out, sewing the patch into place. "Ben, does your family know you've been in the hospital?"

"Why should they?" he growled. Then he kicked the ground with the toe of his foot, and said more evenly, "Dr. Turner wanted to call my parents, but I told him no."

"Do you think that's best?"

Ben jumped at a slithering movement in the grass nearby. When I told him it was just a garter snake, he seemed relieved. But his voice was tight when he said, "I'm not on my parent's insurance anymore, so there's no reason for them to even know I was in the hospital."

"I hope you have some medical insurance," I said.

"That patch gonna work okay?" he asked quickly.

"Sure, it'll be fine." I re-threaded the needle with thin wire. As I pushed the needle through the screen, I went back to the subject of his parents. "Don't you think your folks would want to know? About you being in the hospital?"

He gave me a sharp look, then dropped his gaze and with his good hand banged the pair of wire cutters back and forth against his knee.

I tried to lighten up the discussion. "Where do your parents live?"

"Not far enough away."

"On the mainland?"

At first he didn't answer, but then he muttered, "Bangor. My father's the pastor at Lamp of Faith Church Ministries on Union Street. Pastor Ralph." He grinned, but it was shaky, his lips trembling a little. "Can't you tell I'm a P.K.?"

"P.K.?"

He blushed. "Yeah, preacher's kid. I've been called that all my life. But at least here on Quarry Island nobody calls me that."

When we were finished patching the screen, Ben helped me take care of the tools. "You know," I said, taking the wire cutters he handed me, "I'm getting low on groceries. Maybe we should drive into Hailey's Harbor and pick up a few things at Parson's."

He threw me a glance. "What are you trying to do, adopt me?"

"I'd like you to come along." I didn't say it, but what I really wanted was to prod him back into the real world before he built such a cocoon around himself he wouldn't be able to face the people on the island.

When Ben and I walked into the grocery store, Harry Parson looked up from behind the counter at the tinkle of the bell over the door. I saw him say something to Alvin Sharp who was paying for chewing tobacco. Harry made a motion of tapping the inside of his wrist with his index finger. Alvin nodded, tucked the can of tobacco into his shirt pocket, and walked to the back of the store. He poked at the arm of Julia Whiting, and they bent their heads over the lettuce. Julia glanced over at Ben several times.

I corralled Ben up and down the narrow aisles, asking his suggestions about what kind of soup to buy, whether he liked coconut-covered chocolate doughnuts, if we should get a quart of ginger-ale.

Ben kept his hands in his pockets and his eyes turned away from the other shoppers. He hung close as I wheeled our cart to the check-out counter.

Harry rang up the purchases. "Well, Martha, how ya doing?"

"I'm managing all right."

"Got a friend there with you?" Harry nodded toward Ben.

"You know Ben Gere, don't you? He was here on the island for a while last summer. He's staying at the house up the road from me on Seal Point."

Ben looked away, hiding his injured hand into his jacket pocket.

Harry bagged the groceries, scooping up the cans of tuna, the head of lettuce, the speckled bunch of bananas. "You must be the kid who's painting Owen Tuttle's place."

When Ben stared down at the counter and didn't answer, I put in, "That's right. And he's helping me out too."

I passed one of the bags to Ben. As we walked out of the store, a hush fell behind us, then a swift murmur of voices.

I placed the groceries in the trunk, then slammed it down. Ben went around to the passenger side of the Escort. "I think I should go back to the Tuttle's," he said. "Maybe you could drop me off there."

Ben kept showing up like a stray dog. After moving back and forth between the Tuttle's and my cottage for a few days, he ended up mostly staying at my place. It was just as well. He looked sad, his mouth drawn, his eyes hooded, his shoulders slumped. There was an alarming air of despondency about him, and I didn't think it was a good idea for him to be rambling alone in the big Tuttle house. Even at my place, he kept to himself. He spent hours in his room; he said he was reading, but a few times he left the door ajar and it looked to me that he was just lying on the bed, staring at the ceiling. Other times, he sat on the porch, looking blindly out at the sea. His conversation was clipped and limited, a brief "hi" in response to my "good morning" or a polite "no thank you" when I offered to get him a book from the living room bookcase. He never offered to tell me anything about himself, and he still avoided my eyes when he talked. But he was always well-mannered and really no bother. Having him around helped take my mind off Grace.

When Ben didn't come out of his slump, I thought it was time for him to talk to a professional, so one day I drove him to the clinic. We found Sue outside watering geraniums in clay pots and pansies in window boxes. She wore a sun visor and her usual working uniform: an ankle-length denim dress, white cuff socks, and Bass Weejuns.

"Well, Ben Gere! It's good to see you." Sue set the watering can on the grass and squeezed his shoulders. He turned brick red, dropping his gaze to the ground. Sue looked past him to me. "I'm glad you brought him to see me, Martha." Then she turned her attention back to Ben and said, "Let's all of us go inside."

As we followed her into the waiting room, she pulled off her sun visor and dropped it onto a chair. "Ben, step inside the examining room and I'll take a look at those sutures." And to me, "We won't be long."

In the waiting room, I flicked through an issue of *Time*. Fat Alice lay in the chair next to me, enjoying sunlight that filtered through the open window. I tossed the magazine aside and admired the window box on the other side of the screen. The geraniums framed by the windowsill would make a great photo. The petals were rose-pink, and the leaves looked like little fans catching the light. I scratched Fat Alice behind the ears, and she stretched gratefully.

When Ben came back into the waiting room, he was flexing his fingers and rotating his wrist slowly. "It'll get more flexible as the wound heals," Sue told him, coming up beside him. We were the only people in the waiting room, and I think Sue staged what happened next. I think she wanted me to hear. She took hold of his arms, turning him to face her. "Your wrist looks just fine, Ben, but how are you doing otherwise?"

He shot a glance at me, then blushed as he stared at the carpet. "Good."

"Having any depression?" Sue asked. Fat Alice had slithered off the chair and was rubbing against the back of Sue's legs.

Ben shuffled his feet on the carpet. "Nothing I can't handle."

"Dr. Turner suggested you might want to try an anti-depressant. I can write you an order for Zoloft."

"Nah. I'll be all right." But he didn't sound too sure.

"Why don't you just give it a try? See if it helps the way you feel. You'll need to take it for a few weeks before we can tell if it's working." She pulled a pad out of her pocket of her denim dress. She scribbled a prescription, tore it off, and handed it to him. "And, Ben," Sue went on, "it's important that you talk about what's bothering you. Did you set up any appointments to see Dr. Turner again?"

"We didn't hit it off so good." He looked up at the ceiling, seemed to be studying a water stain near the edge. "I'll be all right," he said again.

The phone rang, and Sue rushed to pick it up before the answering machine kicked in. At the jarring jingle, Fat Alice scurried behind the waiting room chair. Shoving the prescription into his jeans pocket, Ben headed toward the outside door. As I got up to follow him, Sue placed her hand over the receiver and mouthed to me, "Get that filled!"

That evening after supper, I told Ben I had to run into Hailey's Harbor to do a few errands. I left him sitting on the sun porch putting together a jigsaw puzzle, but instead of driving into the village I headed toward the clinic. Sue's house looked warm and inviting to me. I rapped on her door, not knowing if she was home, but she opened it, obviously pleased to see me. But then she said, "Is this a social call? I mean, I hope there's nothing wrong with Ben."

"Well, that's what I wanted to talk to you about. There's no emergency or anything."

"Come in. I'll get out some wine and cheese, and we can talk." She fixed a tray for us, and we moved into her living room. I sat on a flowered loveseat, while Sue sat close-by on the hearth of the unlit fireplace, stroking Fat Alice's fur. "What's on your mind?"

"I guess what I want to know is: how *is* Ben, really?"

She handed me a glass of Chardonnay. "What do you mean?"

I took a sip. "Um, this is nice and dry." I took another sip and set the wine glass on the hearth. "Well, sure, the wound on his wrist is getting better. But what about his mental state? Am I getting in over my head with him?"

"Is he staying with you?" Sue cut into a wedge of Vermont cheddar and handed me a slice sandwiched between Carr's crackers.

"Seems that way. Off and on anyway. He disappears for a few days, goes back to the Tuttle house. Then he shows up on my doorstep again."

"He must feel safe with you," Sue said, slipping a scrap of cheese to Fat Alice. "Have you told him that you read his diary?"

"No. The time hasn't seemed right. Did you?"

"No, I felt the same way. Maybe I'll give Doug Turner a call and see what he suggests about that. Meanwhile, you take the journal with you in case you get the opportunity to discuss it with Ben." She left the room for a minute and came back with the red notebook.

"Weird, huh?" I said as Sue handed it to me. "The stuff Ben writes about?" Fat Alice sniffed my wine, then quickly pulled her head back, her whiskers twitching.

"Well, it gives a pretty clear picture of his state of mind before the suicide attempt." Sue refilled her glass of wine and sat back down on the hearth. "We want to watch him and make sure he doesn't slide back into that kind of thinking. Just keep an eye on him, on his moods."

"Yeah, and while I'm at it I'll save all the orphans in Russia."

Sue smiled at my remark. "Martha, you're not obligated to look after this boy. Don't do more than you want to. You don't owe him anything."

"I know, but he's just a kid. He reminds me of my art students, except he's much more vulnerable. That's what worries me. I'm not sure I know how to help him."

"Just follow your instincts. And let me know if he shows any signs that trouble you."

The crackers and cheese I bit into crumbled into my lap, and I had to use my paper napkin to scoop up the crumbs. Fat Alice leapt to the rescue, lapping up fragments of cheese that had fallen to the floor. "What kind of sign?" I asked.

"Oh, if he obsesses about dying. Makes comments that he'd be better off dead, that kind of thing. Or if he starts to withdraw even more." She reached over with her own napkin and wiped a fleck of cheese off my chin. "You know, the best thing'd be to get him started on the Zoloft."

"I can't force it down his throat." I finished my glass of wine and stood up.

"Well, can you at least convince him to fill the prescription?"

"I'll drive him to the drug store as soon as he agrees," I promised as I went out the door.

When I got back to my cottage, Ben had already settled

into David's room for the night. A strip of light was shining under the bedroom door, so I called out "good night."

In my top dresser drawer, next to the ring I'd found on the beach, I set the red notebook. How stupid of me to take the damn thing in the first place. I should never have become involved. This was *not* how I had planned to spend my summer—babysitting a suicidal teenager. God, I wished Grace were here. She'd know better how to handle the situation. As I got ready for bed, I made a silent pledge not to get in over my head with the Gere boy. He could stay with me if it made him feel safer to have someone around, but I wasn't going to become his personal therapist. I sure as hell wasn't anybody's savior.

For the next few days, I went about my normal day-to-day living. The fall art exhibit was still ahead of me, so I worked on my photography. I shot the boathouse in varying light: early morning, high noon, dusk. I was fascinated with the way shadows on the weathered boards changed as the light shifted.

Ben stayed out of my way for the most part, spending a lot of time in the room he was using, reading a Steven King paperback he'd brought over from the Tuttle house. He was polite, but kept mostly to himself. Once in a while I was able to convince him to go outside for a walk with me, but I noticed that he always avoided going down to the cove. If I suggested we walk down to the cove to beach comb for shells, he would get nervous and hurry back into the cottage.

Each day, he became more moody. Sullen. If he were one of my art students, I'd fail him on attitude alone. Sometimes he'd get a dark look on his face and sit in the living room for

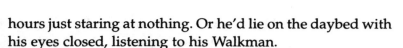

hours just staring at nothing. Or he'd lie on the daybed with his eyes closed, listening to his Walkman.

On the Fourth of July, I went over to Jake and David's for a cookout. Ben wasn't interested in going, so he hung around my cottage all day by himself. That evening, on the way to the village for the fireworks, I stopped by to see if he wanted to join us. He was still lying on the porch daybed, where I'd left him that morning, wearing his headphones. I urged him to go along, but again he refused, so I went on alone because I knew David was waiting for me.

If anything, Ben seemed to be losing ground, sliding into a deeper depression. I was worried. It was time to take Sue's advice, and so the next morning I drove him into Hailey's Harbor.

At The Island Drugstore, Ben reluctantly pulled the Zoloft prescription from his jeans pocket and handed it to the pharmacist behind the counter. Martin Stone smoothed out the crumpled sheet of paper and eyed Ben, who seemed to be gazing at his feet.

"He's a friend of mine, Martin," I said, coming down the aisle. "I was with him when Sue wrote the script."

"Oh, Martha. Hello. Didn't see you there." Martin turned to the rows of medicines and began counting out white pills into a plastic bottle.

"Let's see, that'll be one-oh-five," he said, dropping the bottle into a small bag.

Ben sounded surprised as he said, "One dollar and five cents? That doesn't seem right." At the incredulous look on the pharmacist's face, Ben squeaked, "You don't mean one hundred and five dollars?" He dug out his wallet and found two ten's and a five. Reaching into his front jeans' pocket, he pulled out three wrinkled dollar bills and a quarter. As he counted up what he had, his face turned beet red.

"I didn't know it'd be so much," he stammered.

"Put it on my account, Martin," I offered when I saw the predicament Ben was in.

"I can't let you..." Ben began.

I took the bag from Martin. "Look," I said to Ben, "you can pay me back when the Tuttle's pay you at the end of the summer." As we walked out the door, I suggested to him, "When you need a refill, let's check with Sue and see if she can get her hands on some samples."

We stopped at the hardware store across the street, and I picked up a new latch for the door to my darkroom. Ben bought an inner tube for a bike tire.

Back at my place, I suggested that Ben phone Owen Tuttle and give him a report on the house painting job. While he went inside the cottage to call Florida, I started fixing the door on the shed that Grace and I had converted into a darkroom.

In a short time Ben came back outside and tapped me on the shoulder as I was screwing in the door latch. He handed me a slip of paper on which he'd written the date *July 5* and under that *I owe Martha Felkins $105.00*. It was signed *Ben Gere*.

I nodded and tucked the note into the pocket of my T-shirt. "Did you reach Owen?"

"He was fine about it all. Said to get back to painting when I feel up to it."

Someone from the island must have told Owen what had happened, I guessed. But to Ben I said, "You're ready for it, aren't you?" I thought he should get back to working regularly, have some purpose to his days.

"I suppose."

"How about tomorrow?" I said.

Sure enough, in the morning Ben set out on foot in the direction of the Tuttle house and he was gone all day. Late that afternoon, I was cleaning inside the darkroom when a noise startled me, and I stepped outside. A twelve-speed bike lay in the grass, its wheels still spinning as if someone had just parked it there. As I crossed the yard, I called, "Hello?"

Ben came onto the porch, wearing torn jeans and a stretched out T-shirt which were smeared with paint stains, "Wondered where you were," he said.

"Is that your bike?"

"While I was at Tuttle's, I picked up a few clothes and things. I rode this back."

"So that's what you wanted the inner tube for."

"Yeah. I've got a clunker—an old Bonneville parked in the Tuttle's garage that I was tinkering on before I . . ." He looked down at his wrist. "Well, you know. But biking's cool."

When I stepped onto the sun porch, I noticed a gray gym bag sitting on the floor. "Is that yours?"

"I'll put this in my room." Ben reached for it, then looked up at me, blushing. "I guess I've kind of been taking it for granted I could keep on staying here. You're probably getting tired of me."

Should I assure him that he was welcomed to stay, or should I encourage him to get back to being on his own? To tell the truth, I was ready to have my own space back. But he seemed so needy, I just said, "It's not as lonely with you around."

Ben seemed relieved as he grabbed the gym bag and carried it over the threshold into the house.

He settled in, taking care of the Tuttle house from my place, going over there for most of the day, but showing up again in the late afternoons. A few times when he was gone,

I counted the remaining pills in the Zoloft bottle on the bathroom shelf next to his bag of toiletries. The number of pills was going down, so I assumed he was taking them.

CHAPTER 7

I thought it would be good for Ben to see other people, so I invited Jake and David to dinner. While we waited for the cod to bake, we gathered on the sun porch. On the floor, David thumbed through his fire truck book. Ben sat silently on the daybed with his arms clasped tightly around his waist, avoiding eye contact with anyone.

Jake, never one to pull any punches, was straightforward with Ben. "Are you getting by okay? That wrist of yours mending?" he asked as he leaned against the doorjamb, lifted a pack of Marlboros from the pocket of his flannel shirt, and tapped out a cigarette.

Ben shook his head when Jake offered one to him. "It's coming along."

"Good. That was one wicked cut." Jake struck a match against the edge of the wicker table and lit the cigarette, taking a deep inhale. "When I was a boy your age, I got down on myself too. But after a while you learn to take the good with the bad. Just hang in there. After a spell, you'll figure out it ain't as bad as you think." He glanced over at David,

rocking back and forth on the floor, drool leaking out the corner of his mouth. "When things do turn bad, and you better
believe it can get that way awful fast sometimes, you just bat-
ten down your hatches and plow through the storm."

"Yes, sir," Ben said.

Jake chuckled. "For Chrissakes! Who're you calling *sir*?
You'll make me feel like one of them summer people who
come up here from New York." When he flipped ashes into
the cup of his hand, I pointed to a scallop shell ashtray on
the wicker stand. Jake funneled the ashes into the ashtray,
picked up his open bottle of Bud, and took a deep swig.
Then he asked, "You in the habit of calling people *sir*?"

Ben blushed. "My father . . ."

"Well, I ain't your father. Just call me Jake. Now, David
here, he's called me a lot of things, but he ain't never called
me *sir*. Right, boy?" Jake reached down and wiped the
drool from his son's chin.

David stopped rocking for a moment. "Cap'n Papa."

Jake threw back his head and laughed. "Get up and sit
on that couch there next to Ben. I reckon he's about the
same age as you. The two of you can be buddies."

"You buddy?" David asked, as he plopped down on the
daybed next to Ben. "You my buddy?"

"Take off your hat, boy," Jake said.

But David pulled the floppy red hat further down on his
head and smiled widely at Ben, who smiled back feebly.
David seemed content, sitting quietly next to his new friend,
until his eyes were drawn to the fresh scar on Ben's wrist.
"You man hurt?" He shifted on the daybed, and his eyes got
wide. He yanked off his felt hat and began to twist a strand
of his hair. "You man bleed?" David began chewing his lip.

Ben squirmed on the couch, moving a little away from
David.

I reassured David, "You don't need to worry about Ben. He's much better now. Come on, let's you and me set the table." As I took his hand and helped him up, I said to Jake, "I bet Ben would like to hear about lobster fishing. Tell him about *The Sybil*."

There was nothing Jake liked to talk about more than his boat and the business of fishing. He sat in the wicker chair and turned to face Ben, his elbows on his knees, a beer bottle in one hand. "Fishing's a goddamn mean life, and the best one a man could ask for. Jesus, you oughta hear about the time I got my foot caught in pot warp and damn near got yanked overboard."

I guided David into the kitchen, and he helped put supper on the table. I could hear Jake's booming voice, going on and on about experiences he'd had on his boat. Once in a while, I could hear Ben quietly ask a question or make a comment. Then Jake would start in again with his sea tales until I sent David out to get them.

After the meal, the three of them washed and dried the dishes while I sat at the table finishing a cup of coffee, listening to Jake talk more about fishing. I'd heard his stories so many times, I just kind of tuned him out. But Ben seemed to be eating up his words, and Jake seemed pleased to have such an eager audience.

When he drained the sink, Jake shook soapsuds from his arms and wiped them on the thighs of his jeans. "What do you say we all go out on *The Sybil* for my run tomorrow?"

"Go boat, Papa!" David grinned widely as Jake took a damp dishtowel from him and hung it over the edge of the sink.

Jake said, "You're up to it, ain't you Ben? Of course, that means you gotta haul your ass outta bed real early."

Ben placed a clean dinner plate in the cupboard and

slung his dishtowel over his shoulder. "Yeah, I'd like to come along."

"And you, Martha?" Jake asked, turning to me. "You'll go out with us?"

Caught by surprise, I agreed.

Most of the fishermen moored their boats in Hailey's Harbor, handy to the town wharf and the co-op. But Jake anchored *The Sybil* in deep water at Old Cove and had his own dock where he tied his skiff. Near the dock stood a small fish house for storing gear and repairing traps. Our dad had always tied his boat on the anchor buoy, and as kids, we had been used to looking out the windows of our house, Jake's house now, and seeing his boat sway on its mooring.

I hadn't been aboard *The Sybil* since Grace's accident. When Jake came by to pick up Ben and me before daybreak, I had cold feet and was trying to think of an excuse to stay home. But I couldn't come up with anything and Ben seemed so eager, the most animated I'd ever seen him, that I followed him out to the truck. Jake must have understood that going out on the boat where Grace had died would be a difficult step for me, because he'd insisted on picking us up instead of my driving over to Old Cove.

Jake was at the wheel of his old black Chevy pickup, waiting, the motor running. Both he and David were wearing orange waterproof bib pants and heavy rubber boots. I climbed into the cab next to my brother, while Ben rode in the truck bed with David. Every so often, I glanced back at them through the rear window. Ben was showing the scar on his wrist to David. After a few minutes, Ben put on his green windbreaker and covered the scar with his sleeve. Pulling a small gold pencil-light out of his pocket, he patiently showed David how it worked.

At Old Cove, Jake turned into the driveway, but instead of stopping at his house, he drove past it and continued down the slight incline to the fish house and dock.

When I saw the harbor, my heart jumped. All the memories of last September came rushing back at me.

Grace usually went on a lobster run several times a summer because she liked the way the boat swung in the swells, liked feeling the sea wind on her face and the spray of saltwater. Her dissertation had been on Crane's *The Open Boat*, and she'd presented a few papers on Hemingway's *The Old Man and the Sea*, so I suppose she had a romantic vision of boating.

To me, there was nothing romantic about lobster fishing. I'd been around it all my life. I'd always liked helping my dad on his boat when I was a kid. By the time I'd turned thirteen, I'd saved up enough to buy my own boat—just a 16 footer—and I had a small string of pots too. But it'd never been something I wanted to make a life of. When I'd left the island and moved to the city, I left the life of fishing behind me.

So I didn't go along with Grace when she went aboard Jake's boat for a day's fishing. It was Labor Day. We were leaving for Boston the next day, and I wanted to get the cottage closed up. At dawn, I drove her over to Jake's house. "Look how calm the water is," I said. "Jake won't have to worry about you getting seasick today." That was a private joke between us, because Jake always thought that Grace, being a *city girl* as he called her, would get queasy on the boat. But Grace's stomach, like her spirit, was made of iron.

"I'll come over to pick you up around three," I said as Grace stepped out of the car.

She reached back inside for the jacket on the front seat. She was wearing her fishing hat and an Irish knit sweater. "Don't try to do all the packing yourself," she said. "Leave some for me. I'll help you finish up tonight."

As she stepped back from the car, I nodded and waved, then backed out of Jake's drive. Back at Seal Point, I spent the rest of the day cleaning the cottage and emptying the closets and cupboards.

At three in the afternoon, I bagged up the perishables in the fridge—an opened carton of milk, two sticks of margarine, a nearly full jar of salad dressing, a half dozen eggs, a pound of hamburger—then drove over to Jake's house and put them in his refrigerator. While waiting for *The Sybil* to come in, I sat at his kitchen table, writing out a list of reminders for closing up the cottage:

> *Jake, I think we've taken care of these but please check—*
>   *phone disconnected*
>   *water shut off*
>   *gas off*

Jake's voice coming over the ship-to-shore radio startled me. I stopped writing, cocked my head to listen.

"SOS. *The Sybil*. I'm off Quarry Bank. Headed in to Old Cove. Have medical emergency on board."

The pen fell from my hands when I heard Jake say: "Repeat. Need medical assistance." Then his voice faded out.

My knees trembled as I stood up from the table. What kind of emergency? Had Jake said medical? Had David been in some kind of accident? I heard a siren approaching and looked out the window. Chancey's jeep was tearing down the road. It came to a screeching stop at the fish house, spitting up gravel in its tracks. The sheriff heaved his huge body out of the jeep, then leaned back inside and talked into a mike.

I flung open the front door. Standing on the granite stoop, I shielded my eyes from the sun and scanned the water. *The Sybil* hadn't appeared.

Leaving the door hanging open, I ran. The grass stretched between me and the dock like another ocean. I stumbled several times in the meadow and caught myself to keep from falling. Halfway there, I ran out of breath and had to bend forward with my hands on my thighs.

I raced the rest of the way, reached the edge of the bank, and hurried down the catwalk to the floating wharf. Under me, the tide was rising. At the end of the wharf, I visored my eyes with both hands, leaning into the sun.

Still, there was no sign of *The Sybil*. The floating wharf rocked as Chancey came onto it. I turned to ask him a question, but he pointed toward the water. *The Sybil* was rounding the channel into the cove.

I strained to see who was on board. Jake was at the wheel. And someone on the stern. David.

David flapping his arms.

We watched as the boat chugged across the water. "Where's Grace?" I asked Chancey. Then I yelled, "Jake, where's Grace?"

Jake pulled up to the wharf and cut the engine, tossing a line to Chancey. Then I saw Grace's body crumpled on the deck, her autumn hair tangled with blood, her head at a strange angle. "Oh, my God," I cried, "please don't let this be." I began to climb onto the boat, but Chancey held me back as Jake picked up Grace's body and carried her onto the wharf. Her head hung limp, blood dripping from the back, matted in her hair. Jake laid her on the wharf and the moment I saw her eyes, I knew Grace was dead. Her eyes had always been so full of fire and wit, sparkling like embers in a grate, warm and burning with life. Now they were glazed over and muted. Her wonderful green eyes had changed into the eyes of the dead: snuffed out, veiled.

Clasping Grace's hand, already growing stiff, I collapsed onto the dock and threw my body over her. I touched the face I knew so well, stroked the tangled hair. Pressed my mouth on her lips. Buried my face in the silent chest and wrapped my fingers around the fine gold chain that lay tangled in her sweater. Kneeling on the dock, I screamed, "No! No! No!" The gulls which had followed *The Sybil* to the harbor wheeled into the sky with a mad flurry of wings.

The island ambulance squealed to a stop next to Jake's fish house. Sue and Harold Blume, the volunteer driver, rushed onto the wharf, carrying a stretcher. Jake pried me from Grace's body. "Martha," he choked, "let them do their work." He pulled me to my feet, holding me as Sue checked Grace's chest for a heartbeat, examined her eyes with a small light. She lifted Grace's head and with gloved fingers probed the top of her spine, then examined the cut on the back of her head.

I thought the world had come to an end when Sue drew a white blanket over Grace. In mid-motion she paused, clutching the edge of the blanket and looking down at her old friend. Then she placed it gently over Grace's face. When Sue came over to me and took my elbows, her eyes were wet. "It's too late, Martha. There's no saving her."

My knees went weak. I gasped, covering my mouth with my hand. "My God, Sue, what's happened?"

She wrapped her arms around me and hugged me tightly, not saying anything, just holding me.

Finally, Chancey asked my brother, "How did this happen, Jake?" I pushed away from Sue so I could hear what he said.

Jake answered hastily. "It was an accident. Sure as hell. Gracie slipped. The deck was wet, and she just lost her footing. I saw her fall backward, but hell I just couldn't get to her in time to catch her."

"The injury to her head?" Chancey said. "How'd she get that?"

I stood there in shock as Jake explained, "She come down damn hard, slammed into the edge of the friggin washboard."

"That blow to her head probably killed her at impact," Sue said, wearily pulling the stethoscope from around her neck and folding it into her black bag. Taking the small flashlight out of her pocket, she added that to the bag before closing it. "She's suffered acute head trauma. There's some external bleeding from the wound on the back of her head. But I suspect a broken neck."

My knees buckled at those words, and I sank to the dock. That lovely, lovely neck? The nape with tendrils and wisps of auburn hair, the nape that smelled of lilac perfume, the delicate nape where I often planted kisses? That one? That neck? The one I'd known and loved for twenty years? Broken?

As Chancey and Harold lifted Grace onto the stretcher, Sue put her hand on my arm and said gently, "We'll need you to move back, Martha."

"What are you doing, Sue?" I cried. "Where are you going with Grace?"

"We've got to take her away now, Martha. You know that."

"No. You can't," I wailed.

Jake reached down to help me up, but Sue stopped him. "That's okay. We can wait a few more minutes," she said, her voice choked.

I sat on the dock next to the stretcher and pulled back the blanket from Grace's face. Slipping my arm under her shoulders, I lifted her toward me, holding her in my arms, rocking her, kissing her forehead, her cheek. "Dear one, dear one," I moaned, "don't leave me. Come back."

Sue gripped my shoulder. "Martha, I know this is hard, but we have to take her now."

I looked up at my friend and saw tears in her eyes. Numbly, I nodded, then laid Grace's head on the stretcher. I gave her one last kiss on the lips, but I couldn't draw the blanket over her face.

Jake pulled me to my feet and held his arm tightly around me as Chancey and Harold loaded the stretcher into the ambulance. Harold climbed into the driver's seat, and Sue got in on the other side. They drove off, carrying Grace away, with Chancey following in his jeep. I watched them inch up the incline toward Granite Road and disappear around the corner.

Just then Jake dropped his arm from around my shoulders and called out, "David, keep still! Settle down!"

David, standing in the cockpit of the boat, was flapping one hand in front of him; it jerked about like an injured bird. With his other hand he kept pulling his hair.

"David, quit that!" Jake snapped again, panic in his voice.

Ignoring his father, David began to turn in circles on the deck. Turning. Pulling his hair. Crying and laughing hysterically, a choked yipping noise escaping from his mouth.

Jake left me and stepped onto the boat to calm David. Alone now on the dock, I looked down at my hand. My knuckles were smudged with Grace's blood, and her gold necklace was wrapped around my fingers. But the pendant —the heart and pearl—was missing.

Now, nine months later, I was back where I'd lost Grace, wondering why in the world I was doing this. Why was I going out on Jake's boat? Why did I even come back to this island? As I sat in the truck and stared numbly at the harbor, Jake patted my leg. "Come on, sis. Let's get it over with." He squeezed my knee, then reached past me and pushed open my door.

David had already jumped out of the back and was standing by the truck door. He yanked my hand excitedly, his face glowing. "Marfa, come boat."

Jake went inside the fish house and brought out orange oilskin bibs and black rubber boots for Ben. He tossed him a pair of gloves. "Here, put these on." As Jake carried buckets, a mended trap, and line from the fish house down to the dock, Ben was quick to help.

Jake dinghied out to his mooring, standing up as he rowed. He tied the small rowboat to his mooring and jumped onto the bow of the larger boat. *The Sybil* was a thirty-three foot, diesel-powered, wood boat with a high bow and a low stern. She was navy blue with white trim, and her deck and washboard were painted gray. She had a small cabin for stowing gear and a wheelhouse with instruments: depth finder, fuel gauges, VHF radio. A CB radio hung overhead. The port side of the wheelhouse was enclosed. Over the open starboard side swung a hydraulic pot hauler; the steering station was close by so Jake could steer and work the pot-hauler at the same time. From the top of the pilothouse rose antennas, an exhaust pipe, and one of Jake's blue-and-white pot buoys. The sides of the boat were low with a washboard for resting lobster traps as they were emptied or baited.

Starting the engine, its low rumble echoing across the water, Jake maneuvered *The Sybil* back to the dock. Welcomed by the sharp smell of diesel fuel and herring bait, we jumped aboard, and David cast off the dock lines. From his post in the wheelhouse, Jake shifted the engine into gear and navigated around moored lobster boats, the pale light of dawn spreading over the still sea.

As we chugged toward the mouth of the harbor, I sat in a webbed lawn chair in the stern, watching the wake behind the transom churning like waves of my own emotions. Ben stood next to Jake, listening as Jake explained how to navigate the boat. "We'll keep that nun to our port," he was saying, pointing ahead and to the left at a red channel marker. "Remember the rule: red, right, return. Now, when we get out of the harbor, we'll head straight out to the grounds. Got four hundred pots in all, but we ain't gonna haul 'em all today. Right, David?"

David, who was standing in the cockpit next to two barrels of salted herring, answered, "Yep, Cap'n Papa."

Once we passed the no-wake buoy, Jake pushed the throttle full ahead. I could feel the vibrations of the noisy engine, and my body rocked with the boat as we cut through the sea. Suddenly, I had trouble catching my breath as images of Grace came rushing at me. I pictured her standing here in the cockpit, laughing and talking. Then I saw her fall, but I didn't see what made her fall. I suppose her arms flailed as she tried to catch her balance. There must have been a terrible whack as her head slammed against the washboard, her neck striking the brass coaming. I imagined her sliding limply, the shocked look in her green eyes, the blood matting her faded auburn hair, her head lolling like a rag doll. Then her body was lying grotesquely twisted in the slime of the wet deck. A shudder ran over me, a chill. I couldn't bear to think of that day.

The engine shifting down brought my attention back to the present. Jake slowed near a blue-and-white lobster buoy, his color pattern. Many of his buoys floated near us.

"How'd you know where to go?" Ben asked.

"Mostly, I use landmarks, like that cove over there, to tell where I'm at. I outta know it, been fishing here all my life," Jake explained as he idled the engine. "There's lots of ridges under here where the lobsters like to hide out. These were my dad's grounds before me. That's how they go, father to son."

"Or daughter, if she's interested," I piped up.

Jake insisted, "Most times it's a boy." He glanced over at David, who was standing near the bait barrel, studying a metal buckle on the straps of his oilskin bibs. "Anyhows," Jake went on, "I know these grounds like the back of my hand." Jake reached over the side with a gaff and hooked the floating buoy, then looped the buoy's warp into a hydraulic pot hauler that was suspended over the starboard side. When he switched on the pot hauler, it whirred, pulling the trap from the ocean. Coiling rapidly at his feet, the warp splashed Jake and Ben and the deck around them. Soon a wire trap emerged, salt water and seaweed dripping from it, starfish and snails clinging to it. "Grab ahold of that and set it on the rail," Jake told Ben, who grabbed the trap and pulled it onto the washboard. Following that, another trap emerged, and Ben pulled that beside the first one.

"I always used to have wood pots," Jake told Ben. "But I been changing over to these new wire traps. Some guys say they catch more fish. I wouldn't swear to that, but they ain't as much upkeep, and they last longer. Besides, they're easier to stack and a hell of a lot lighter than the old ones." He slipped off the bungee cords that kept the lids closed, then quickly sorted though the blackish-green lobsters, flinging a couple of obvious shorts overboard. After immobilizing the claws of several others with rubber bands, he tossed them into a plastic tub full of circulating water.

"Gotta measure this one," Jake said, showing Ben how to check the length of the carapace with a bronze gauge. "It's just under, so we gotta put it back and let it grow some more." He spun the lobster through the air, and it splashed into the bottle-green sea.

Lifting a last lobster out of the traps, Jake said, "This one's a notched female. We'll put her back too. She's part of the breeding stock."

I didn't remember ever seeing Ben so interested in anything. He was eagerly watching every move Jake made. "How'd you tell it's female?"

"Sometimes you see berries on her belly, eggs that is." Jake pointed to the tail with the blade of his jackknife. "But this one here's marked. See where someone's already notched the flipper, second one on the left?" He pitched the thrashing lobster overboard.

Turning the traps upside down, first one, then the other, Jake shook them over the side of the boat to empty them of crabs and urchins. "Clean out those old bait bags," he told Ben, "and give them to David so he can fill them for the next set of traps. Get a couple fresh ones from him." As Ben tossed the scraps overboard, seagulls screamed and dove and fought for the discarded bait.

David had already filled two bags with herring and hung them on the rim of the bait barrel; he eyed Ben sullenly as he grabbed them from the rim. Jake showed Ben how to put these fresh bait bags into the traps, then fastened the lids with the bungee cords and set the traps on the washboard. The boat pulled away as Jake hit the throttle, and the empty traps were dumped one by one overboard, the warp on the deck humming as it trailed them.

After filling the empty bait bags and hanging them on the rim, David stood near the barrel, his shoulders slumped, his legs spread on the deck to balance himself against the rocking of the boat. He seemed to be guardedly observing his father at the wheel as he moved the boat toward the next string. David especially seemed to be watching Ben, who was standing at Jake's side.

The morning wore on. Jake idled the engine each time traps were hauled, emptied of lobsters, freshened with bait, and dumped back overboard. Then he would gun the throttle and speed to the next set of traps, hoping to pull as many as he could in a day. Meanwhile, the CB radio squawked with chatter from other lobsterman at sea.

Around noon, when the sun was hot overhead, we took a brief break to eat the lunch Jake had packed for us: crabmeat sandwiches creamy with mayonnaise, Saltine crackers with peanut butter, and cans of Coke. Then Jake continued working his way along his fishing grounds.

All the while, David was unusually quiet, filling bait bags when needed and hanging them on the rim of the barrel. He kept glancing up from his work, keeping an eye on his father as Jake taught Ben how to do the work of sternman.

Around three in the afternoon, we tied up to the lobster car. Jake put his catch in the storage crate that floated under water, explaining to Ben what he was doing. David stood sulking, his hand braced overhead on the edge of the wheelhouse roof, while he watched the two of them. As we neared Old Cove, he hosed down the cockpit.

When we came into the dock at Old Cove, Jake slid into the dock and swung the bow around, then kicked it into reverse to bring the stern alongside. David used a gaff to catch a ring on the dock, and he made fast the mid-ship line. But then he refused to get out of the boat.

"C'mon, boy, climb out," Jake said. David shook his head vigorously, refusing to look at his dad. He stared at his boots. Jake tried another tack, a joking tone to his voice: "Captain Papa orders everyone off the ship!"

Still, David wouldn't move. Catching Jake's attention, I placed my finger on my nose and tapped the bridge. "Out of joint," I whispered.

Jake understood my meaning. "Martha, you and Ben get off here. It ain't too far for you to walk home, is it? Me and David gotta run over to Hailey's Harbor and buy some bait at the co-op. Ain't that right, pal?"

David made a swatting motion with his hand, urging Ben and me to get off the boat. "You go. I help Cap'n Papa."

CHAPTER 8

The whole island was socked in with fog, the foghorn bleating forlornly. Closing the door between the porch and the kitchen, I said to Ben, "It's too damp to paint today. A good morning for burrowing in with a book."

I pointed out the choice of magazines, paperbacks, and hardcovers in the low bookcases that lined the living room walls. But Ben produced a thumb-worn copy of *Carrie* from his room. For myself, I picked out a biography of Dorothea Lange, which I had already read many times. After I lit a fire to take the edge off the chill, I settled into the wing chair by the fireplace, while Ben sat in the thick-cushioned rattan chair. We turned on the lamps.

When I looked up from my book an hour or so later, Ben was staring at the dying fire. "Tired of reading?" I asked.

My voice startled him, and he bolted from the chair. He went over to the fireplace and jabbed at the embers with an iron poker. Then he put another log on the fire and watched as it caught and flamed. Leaning against the pine mantel, he rubbed absentmindedly at the mole on his forehead, still staring at the flames.

"What are you so deep in thought about?" I asked.

He jumped. "Nothing," he mumbled as he brushed again at the mole, this time with his knuckles. He went back to the chair, slouched into it, and dropped his feet on the ottoman; the heels of his Reeboks sunk into the faded floral cushion.

"Are you hungry?" I asked. "You could put the kettle on for tea. Make yourself some toast."

"Don't worry about me."

"I do worry, Ben." I slipped a bookmark inside the pages and set my book on the end table. "Look, in all these weeks we've never really talked. You know, about why you hurt yourself that day on the beach. Maybe it's time we got it all out in the open."

He shrugged, rubbing the knees of his jeans.

"That's what I miss most about Grace," I said. "Having her here to talk to."

"Yeah." He studied the tips of his fingers and picked at a hangnail.

Talking to him was like talking to a wall, except I wouldn't expect a response from a wall. *To hell with it*, I thought, *just dive right in*. I went into my bedroom and came back with his red notebook. "Ben," I said, handing it to him, "you should know that I read this."

"What?" Surprise flashed across his face, and for once he looked right at me. "Where'd you get this?"

I had his attention now. "I should have told you before. It's not like me to snoop in someone else's private things. But while you were in the hospital, I found your notebook at the Tuttle house. It was right there on the kitchen table. And it seemed to me that maybe you meant for it to be found."

The expression on his face moved from surprise to anger, blotches of red spreading on his cheekbones. "Fuck!" He grabbed the notebook from my hand. "I can't believe you'd do that."

"I should have told you right away. But I wasn't sure. I just wanted to do what was best."

"What makes you think you know what's best for me? You're not my mother," he snapped as he started to get up from the chair. Then he slumped back and tossed the notebook onto the ottoman in front of him. "Fuck it, anyway."

"Look," I said, "we've got two choices. We can pretend I never read your diary and try to go on like we were before. Or we can talk about it and get it out in the open."

"Whatever." He sat with his forehead pressed against his hands.

Kneeling on the floor in front of him, I pulled his hands from his face and was surprised to find that he was weeping. Holding his hands I whispered, "I'm so sorry about the things that happened to you. All that you've been through."

He muttered something I couldn't hear.

"What?" I asked gently. "What did you say, Ben?"

"I wish I'd died. Wish you and Jake had stayed out of the fucking way."

"None of it was your fault, you know. What your father did to you," I said gently. "He's the only one to blame for that. Not you." Ben swabbed his eyes with the back of his hands, then turned away from me. I returned to my chair, tiredly resting my head against the upholstered back. Why had I taken this on?

I was surprised when Ben broke the silence. His voice was halting, almost inaudible. "My old man, my father . . ."

Closing my eyes, I nodded, hoping to encourage him.

He stammered, "I c-c-can't explain him. He's a fucking p-p-power freak. Thinks he's in charge of my life."

I nodded again to let him know I was listening.

"Everything's got to be his way. Which he passes off as God's way," Ben snorted, kicking the ottoman over onto the braided rug, his notebook falling open beside it.

I waited until it became obvious that he wasn't going to say anything more. Then I set the ottoman back on its feet, closed the notebook, and placed it on top of the flowered footstool. Ben sat hunched over in his chair, his blond hair hanging over his eyes. When I reached down to push the hair from his forehead, he flinched.

It was obvious Ben was through talking. I left him to brood in his chair. I felt drained, tired of dealing with a sulky teenager. We both needed some space.

The morning was still young as I crossed the lawn, but the fog was lifting, drifting in wisps instead of hanging in a dense curtain as it had earlier. I lifted the latch to the shed, dampness following me in. I'd always found sanctuary in a darkroom. During the school year I used the facilities at the Art Institute. I kept my photos in my campus office, too, for the most part, catalogued and marked. But it was also necessary to have a place to develop film here on the island, since I often did free-lance projects in the summer. One year I'd had a calendar assignment to shoot black-and-white photographs of Down East lighthouses. I'd traveled up and down the coast, setting my tripod on the ledges at Pemaquid, shooting the Nubble light, filming the Green's Head Light on Quarry. Another year, Bumble Bee had hired me to shoot pictures of the tuna tournament in Mackerel Cove. This summer I would prepare prints for the exhibit coming up in Boston.

Grace and I had converted the shed into a darkroom, doing most of the work ourselves. We'd hired Island

Electric to run electricity from the main power box and Clarence Potts Plumbing to install running water. But she and I did all the rest: light-proofing, putting in ventilation, laying the flooring, and hammering tables and shelves. We divided the space into two areas: a wet area for mixing chemicals and processing film, and a dry bench for selecting negatives and exposing paper.

Now I happily puttered around my worktable, wiping down the enlarger and other equipment. It was a relief just to be by myself and not have to sidestep around Ben's moods. Let him sit in the house and mope, if that's what he wanted.

At first when I spotted the two canisters of undeveloped film, I couldn't quite believe it. I'd been looking for them all winter, tearing my apartment apart looking for them. Now, here they were, a little dusty but intact. Evidently, they'd rolled into the corner of the worktable, and in my rush to get away last fall—and in my state of shock—I'd left them behind. My heart jumped as I picked up the canisters and juggled them in my hand. If they were the pictures I thought they were, I couldn't wait to process them. I had to see those images.

But first I needed developing fluid and printing paper.

The thought of going over to the mainland alone was very appealing. But when I went back into the cottage, there was Ben still in the rattan chair, staring at the dying fire. I couldn't let him just sit around like a lump all day— it wasn't good for him. Maybe a change of scenery would shake him out of his doldrums. I gave up the idea of a trip alone, no matter how tempting it was, and invited him to come along.

Somehow, I convinced him. Maybe he caught some of my enthusiasm. Or maybe he was just tired of sitting around, feeling sorry for himself.

As we walked onto the ferry late that morning, I carried a small backpack for the photo supplies I planned to buy. The first two ferry runs had been canceled because of the fog, so the eleven-fifteen was crowded.

Ben and I managed to find a seat inside the cabin on the lower deck. The fog had vanished but left a gray drizzle in its place. I was wearing my blue windbreaker over a cable-knit sweater, and still felt chilly. Over his sweatshirt Ben was wearing a green windbreaker, and on his head was a Red Sox baseball cap. We didn't talk much during the crossing, just drank hot coffee from our thermos as we watched our progress through Penobscot Bay.

After the ferry landed in Rockland and we were walking off the ramp, I took a risk with Ben. "Do you think it'd be a good idea to take a cab to Pen Bay and see if you can talk with Dr. Turner?" I asked him on an impulse. "We have time, if you want to. If he's busy, maybe you can set up an appointment."

He scowled. "Don't need to."

"Didn't Dr. Turner tell you to check in with him once in a while?"

Ben jammed his hands into the pockets of his windbreaker.

It was a hopeless cause. He was not interested in seeing the hospital psychiatrist. I should just give it up. But I said, "Well, I hope you'll at least see Sue again soon."

"I thought you came here to buy something," he said.

We strolled along Main Street, stopping at a few of the stores. We spent quite a bit of time in Second Read Books. I found an old copy of Rachel Carson's *The Sea Around Us*, and Ben picked up a Richard Straub paperback for 25 cents. We walked over to Elm Street and visited the Farnsworth Art Museum to look at the Wyeth paintings. When we crossed back to Main Street, we went into PDQ, the photography store where I'd been getting supplies every summer for years. I bought Kodak printing paper, processing chemicals, and bulk black-and-white film, which I packed in my knapsack.

As we left the PDQ, I asked, "What do you say we grab an early supper? I'll treat you for coming along with me today. The Rockland Café, just down the street here, makes great lobster rolls."

When the waiter at the café brought our sandwiches with a Pepsi for Ben and a cup of mint tea for me, Ben blurted out, "I never even tasted lobster until I was a freshman in high school."

"You must be joking. Living right near the coast all your life? I'd have thought you would have had it often."

Ben bit into a potato chip. "My parents did," he said, picking up another chip. Our relaxed afternoon together had made him unusually talkative. "One of the men from the fellowship, Brother Frank, runs a fish shop in Bangor and a couple of times a summer he gives my father some live lobsters. Three of them. My father lets my mother have one—her tip for cooking them, I guess—but he eats the other two himself."

"You don't get any?"

Ben shrugged as he took a huge bite of his sandwich.

"What did you eat when your parents had lobster?"

He answered with his mouth full, his words muffled. "A hot dog. Or tomato soup and crackers." He wiped his lips with the back of his hand. "I was used to eating different from them. My father said it was good discipline for me. Same thing when they had steak, or pork chops, or roast. I'd get grilled cheese. Maybe a bowl of oatmeal. My mother made me a lot of peanut butter-and-jelly sandwiches."

"That would've made me mad as hell," I said.

Ben stuffed a handful of potato chips into his mouth and took a swig of Pepsi. "I learned pretty quick it didn't do any good to complain, so I just kept quiet and ate what they gave me." He took another big bite of his sandwich.

I sat back and sipped my tea. When he finished, I made a motion for the waiter and said, "Ben, you're going to eat as many damn lobster rolls as I can afford."

During the ferry ride home, we polished off the coffee in our thermos while we shared the *Bangor Daily News*. I was reading the sports page, an article about the LPGA Open, when Ben poked me with his elbow.

He shook out the Religion page of the newspaper and pointed at a press release in the lower left corner. The bold headline caught my eye: *Revivals*. I leaned closer and read:

> *Bangor—An Old-Fashioned Revival with Evangelist Bobby Blessing, hosted by Pastor Ralph Gere. 11 a.m. and 6 p.m., Sunday, July 16. 7 p.m. Monday through Thursday, July 17-20. Lamp of Faith Church Ministries, 1500 Union Street. Call 945-5555.*

"Aren't you impressed?" Ben made a hard little laugh as he carefully folded the sheet of newspaper, burying the article. He kept folding it into smaller pieces, making very sharp and precise creases, ironing the paper with his hands.

"Your father?" I asked. "Pastor Ralph?"

"You should see him at those revival meetings. It's a real party. He's just jumping with news of Jesus." His eyes narrowed as he pressed the page into a tight, little square.

"He's a hypocrite," I said. "If I were you, I'd never want to have anything to do with a man like that again, even if he was my father."

Ben didn't make any response, just grunted.

"What are you going to do with that?" I asked, pointing to the wad of newspaper clenched in his fist.

"Flush it down the fucking toilet."

"I've got a better idea. One that won't plug up the plumbing." I rolled the rest of the newspaper and held it up like a torch. "Let's make a damn good bonfire."

We waited until dusk before we lit a fire in the brick pit on the front lawn. Together we burned the entire newspaper, crinkling each page and tossing it into the fire.

Ben sat in one of the Adirondack chairs and watched intently as each page darkened, burst into flames, floated up in black flakes, then drifted down into gray ash. He saved the article about his father for last. With great deliberation, he unfolded the wad of paper, spread it on the grass, and rubbed the heel of his hand over it. Ripping the page into minute pieces, he dropped them one by one into the flames. Long after the paper disintegrated, he sat stroking the scar on his wrist and staring into the fire. Finally, without a word, he stood up and went inside the cottage.

I sat outside and waited for the fire to burn down. The surf shushed against the rocky shore, a few fireflies flitted by, a cloud moved over the moon. I pulled my sweater more tightly around me. I'd left the light on in my bedroom, and June bugs thudded against the screen, trying to get in.

The next morning, as soon as Ben rode off on his bike for the Tuttle house, I headed for the darkroom. He'd be painting all day and not get back until late afternoon. I had the whole day to myself.

Now that I had fresh photo supplies, I couldn't wait to process the two rolls of film I'd found. I'd been afraid that film was lost for good, and now here it was. I developed the negatives and hung them to dry, weighted with clothespins. My hands shaking in anticipation, I looked closely at the negatives with a magnifying glass. Yes! They were pictures of Grace! Pictures I'd taken last summer, just before her accident.

Cutting the negatives into strips, I made contact prints and clipped those up to dry. Again, I studied those with a magnifying glass, relishing in Grace's image, deciding which ones to enlarge. I wanted to start printing right away.

Absorbed in my work, I spent the rest of the day processing: exposing individual negatives under the enlarger, then sliding the print into the developer tray, lifting it with a pair of tongs to the stop bath, using another set of tongs to transfer it to the fixer. I washed the prints under running water, wiped off the excess with a squeegee, hung them to dry, until 8 X 10 prints of Grace were suspended over the whole darkroom. Images of her hovered all around me, like black-and-white celestial spirits.

From the very beginning, I loved taking Grace's photo. I took pictures of her every chance I had. I couldn't get enough of looking through the lens at her, then in the darkroom watching her face appear as I developed the film.

But over the years, as Grace grew older, she became surprisingly self-conscious about her appearance. Whenever I pulled out a camera, she'd brush me off. "Stop that, now. Who wants to see pictures of a baby-boomer dyke?" When I insisted, telling her she looked just as beautiful as ever, she said. "Look at me. My throat's getting wrinkled as a turkey's. See here," she said, pointing to the back of her hand, "age spots. It was bad enough when it was just freckles. Now it's all these other gross brown spots, too."

I kept after her, though, and one day toward the end of last summer she'd given in and let me photograph her.

On that late August day, I woke up just after dawn. Grace's side of the bed was empty. As soon as I dressed, I went looking for her. She was outside, slipping on a pair of gardening gloves. "There you are. You're up early," I said.

"Oh, hi. Couldn't sleep anymore, so I thought I'd get at this job." She knelt down on the grass and began to weed around the mums. Watching her from the steps of the sun porch, I noticed how the rosy dawn light bounced off her face and arms. The rays of the rising sun highlighted the red of her hair, which over the last few years had begun to fade.

Quickly, I stepped into the cottage and loaded a Nikon, then I hurried back outside. Standing on the porch steps, I shot down at her. Click, click, click. Then I stepped down on the grass next to her, crouching on the ground, circling her, snapping the shutter. Bracing the camera on the arm of the small apple tree, I clicked, cocked the shutter, clicked again.

At first Grace seemed annoyed. "Do you really have to do that?" she asked.

"Oh, come on, humor me this once," I said, clicking away.

She shook her head, but soon she was involved with weeding again and didn't pay much attention to me as I kept on shooting.

After I finished that roll of film, I suggested we go inside for more pictures.

"Are you kidding? I just started here. I want to keep on with it," she said as she pulled up a thistle and tossed it onto the grass.

"Come on Grace. Just for me?" I pleaded as I pulled her sleeve.

She looked up at me, and I gave her the best smile I could work up that early in the morning. "This is downright silly," she said, but I sensed she was weakening.

"Look, sweetheart, do this for me," I coaxed, "and I'll make you a nice breakfast. Mushroom-and-green pepper omelet? Toast with orange marmalade?"

"That's hard to resist," she grinned, then she followed me inside. Grace took off her gardening gloves and washed her hands in the kitchen sink, while I reloaded the camera. Then I walked around the rooms trying to find the best light. In the bedroom I noticed how the morning sun slanted through the window so that the lace curtains made a design on the bed. I wanted to see those pinpoints of light and shadow playing over Grace.

I smoothed the chenille bedspread over the sheet. "Lie down here, this has the best light."

"I just got up from there a little while ago," she complained.

"It won't take long. I promise."

"You know, you're really impossible sometimes." Kicking off her gardening sneakers, she stretched out on her back.

It was when I said "take off your clothes" that she got upset.

"Don't be ridiculous." She raised up on one elbow. "I agreed to a few quick photos. You didn't tell me you wanted nude pictures."

"Just a few. Nobody'll ever see them except us."

"You're serious about this, aren't you?"

"It'll make a great shot. Trust me." I set up the tripod and screwed the camera onto the base. When I finished, I looked up to find Grace hadn't removed her clothes. "Need help?" I asked, moving to the bed. I started to unbutton her blouse, but she put her hand over mine. Leaning down, I blew hot air onto her neck, then licked the path to her cleavage, working my tongue around the chain with the heart-and-pearl pendant.

She sighed. "You did say an omelet, right?"

"Um hum. And toast. Hash browns, if you want them." She let me unbutton her blouse. I slipped it off, kissing her shoulder. When I started to unfasten the clasp of the necklace around her neck, she stopped me.

"I'll keep that on."

"Okay," I said, so I moved down her back and unfastened her bra, letting it drop onto the bed. I removed her slacks and panties, then gathered all her clothes and set the bundle on the antique trunk at the foot of the bed.

Crouched behind the camera, I focused the lens. "That's great. Wonderful," I said as I clicked the shutter. "Mmm, baby, I like what I see."

"How can you like this old body?" Grace protested. "I'm all wrinkles and soft flab."

I lifted my eyes from the camera. "That's not true. And even if it were, what difference would it make?" Bending over, I peered through the viewfinder again. This time, Grace was more relaxed and looked directly at the camera. After shooting about half a roll, I asked her to roll over onto her stomach. Lacy shadows danced across her back, over the curve of her ass, on her freckled breasts that rounded beneath her arms. Shooting quickly, I finished the roll of film.

When I stopped, Grace turned onto her side, facing me, and curled up her knees. "Happy now?" she asked.

"Yes, thank you," I said as I folded the tripod and packed the camera into the bag. When I looked up again, Grace's eyes were closed and she looked so lovely in the morning light. Undressing quickly, I tossed my clothes onto the black trunk and lay down next to her.

Grace's eyelids fluttered and opened. "I'm waiting for breakfast," she said.

"Let's have something sweet for the first course," I whispered as I cupped her breast with my hand and circled her nipple with my tongue.

Now Grace was gone. All I had were these pictures of her. When the photos dried, I thumb-tacked them to the bare wood walls of my bedroom, adorning the room with her. I would sleep better from now on, because her face would be the last thing I saw when I closed my eyes at night and the first to greet me in the morning.

As the days passed, I grew used to having Ben around. I told Sue over the phone that the Zoloft seemed to be helping, because his mood was lighter. Instead of moping around inside the cottage all day, muffled from the world with his headphones, Ben was holding down two jobs. He'd seemed so interested in the boat that Jake asked him to work with him and David on *The Sybil*. My feeling was that Jake thought being on the sea would be good for him. Whatever the reason, every day now Ben rode his bike over to Old Cove before daybreak to go fishing. When they came in from hauling traps in the afternoon, he biked over to the Tuttle's to scrape and paint the house.

I was afraid David would be jealous of Ben working on *The Sybil*. But he took to him. In fact, now whenever David stopped by my cottage in the evening or on the weekend, he'd holler, "Where my Bennybuddy?" before he was even onto the porch. Ben found an old basketball hoop, minus the netting, on the island dump and carried it home on his bicycle. He made a backboard for it and nailed it to a post in my yard. Once he had the net up, he taught David to shoot baskets. David held the ball with both hands between his legs, and when he heaved it into the air, his whole body rocked backward. At first, he got irritable when he missed and would stomp the ground with his foot. He'd picked up some colorful language from Jake and the other fisherman at the wharf, and he'd bellow, "Shit-a-damn!" or "Chrissake!" But Ben was always patient with him, standing behind him and guiding his arms until David finally learned how to aim the ball into the hoop. Now David seldom missed, and when he made a shot he always swung around and gave a high-five to Ben.

CHAPTER 9

Preparing for the Guild of Boston Artists' show that was scheduled to open in October took up a lot of my days. I envisioned a grouping of photos: a close-up of a shell, or driftwood, or a sea rose, each closely cropped—sort of *Georgia O'Keefe at the Seashore*. In the course of my career, I'd found that black-and-white photography could translate the complex play of light and reveal the essential form of a subject, so that was the medium I was using. I was never happier than when I was doing photography work. Most days while Ben was off fishing with Jake or painting the Tuttle house, I was shooting film around the island, exploring close-up nooks and crannies I'd known all my life, attempting to get a fresh scrutiny of the smallest objects. My work was at a point where I needed to move into the darkroom.

The air in the shed was close and stuffy, so I set up a fan. I'd already made contact prints of the negatives I'd shot on the beach below my house at the first of the summer, so I decided to work on those first. I used a magnifying glass to scrutinize the contact prints, looking for frames that interested me artistically because of composition, contrast in light and dark, or sharpness. I hoped to find some shots that would meet my standards so I could print and mount them for the exhibit.

The frame of the eyeless seagull was startling and strong. The ones of the horseshoe crab were disappointing; the depth of field wasn't right. There was a shot of tangled kelp and barnacles that might work. Another of periwinkles. I especially liked one of a lobster buoy that had washed up on the beach, a short piece of waterlogged line hanging from it.

My eyes skimmed over a frame that seemed soft in focus, then moved on to the next one. But something jogged my mind, so I looked again at the previous frame. It was a shot of a gull's feather lying in the sand and something circular and shiny that I couldn't quite make out. I looked more closely, holding the magnifying glass and squinting. Of course. That was what turning fifty did for you—my memory was getting worse every day.

The picture was of Ben's ring, the one I'd found on the beach the day after Ben hurt himself. The ring I'd never told him about. I'd almost forgotten I had the damn thing. I should have given him that ring when I handed him the notebook. Get it all over with at once.

The first subject I picked to enlarge was the seagull. I switched off the overhead light, and that magical moment of complete darkness descended with its familiar smell of chemicals. Bathed in the red safelight, I exposed the negative, dodging and burning to get the effect I wanted. When the exposure was complete, I slid the print into the developing tray, using tongs to transfer it to the stop bath, then to the fixer. With a wash in running water and a wipe of the squeegee, the print was ready to be clipped up to dry.

As I repeated the process with other frames, I included the shot of Ben's ring, enlarging and cropping closely. Then, with the prints hung to dry, I closed the door to the dark-room, flipping the hook over the new latch.

It was one of those unusual days on the Maine coast when the air was humid and uncomfortable, so I carried the fan into the cottage and set it up.

In my bedroom dresser, I found Ben's ring under a T-shirt. I slipped it onto my thumb and twirled it around. It really was just a cheap, lightweight, gold-colored band. Just then, a truck drove into the yard, and I quickly dropped the ring into the pocket of my shorts. Someday I'd tell Ben I had it, when the time was right.

With a great ruckus, all three men came onto the porch and then into the house. "Get a move on, Martha! We're all going out to supper," Jake shouted. Even in this heat he was wearing a flannel shirt, though he did have the sleeves rolled up above his elbows.

"What are you talking about?" I met them in the kitchen.

Jake shook a Marlboro from a pack. "There's a pollack feed at The Seagull's Nest. Every living soul in town'll probably be there, and that means us too. Right, boys?" He tamped the cig-arette on the cellophane pack, then lit it with a kitchen match.

"Yep!" David excitedly tugged at the red felt hat that sat like a tent on his head. Sweat ran down his face.

"David, take that hot thing off." I reached for the hat.

"No, Marfa!" He grabbed the brim with both hands, yanking it further down on his head.

"Look, I'm not wearing my hat." Ben lifted off his Red Sox cap and hung it on a peg beside the front door. "See, dude? It's not cool to wear hats when we go out to a restaurant."

David pulled off his own hat and hung it over Ben's. His thin patchy hair was pasted to his forehead.

"Let's run a comb through that," I said, taking David's hand and leading him toward the bathroom. When he started to balk, Ben followed us in, pulled a small black comb from his own back pocket, leaned into the mirror that hung over the counter, and began fixing his own hair. Then David was eager to comb his hair too, but he didn't want any help. We left him in the bathroom and when he came out later with his hair parted in the middle and a cowlick standing up, he looked so proud nobody said anything.

The Seagull's Nest was packed, so we had to wait on the sidewalk outside the restaurant. The village buzzed with people. As Jake had said, everyone in town, including a handful of tourists, seemed to have come out for the pollack dinner. At the side of the restaurant, I leaned against the steel railing of the bridge, its green paint flaking and exposing rust. The incoming tide frothed in the raceway where water rushed under the bridge into a deep tidal pool.

"I go swim, Marfa," David said, leaning over the railing.

"Oh no, you don't." I quickly grabbed the back of his shirt. "Stop that, David!"

"I fool you!" He grabbed both my hands, swinging them. "I kid Marfa."

"Don't ever do that again, David! It's not safe. See how fast the tide comes in under the bridge. It's very, very dangerous."

From the restaurant door, Jake motioned for us to come inside, calling out that a table was ready. As the four of us walked through the small crowded dining room, Jake stopped at Harry Parson's table, "It's hotter than a witch's how-do-you-do, ain't it, Harry?" Then he waved to Clarence Potts sitting by the window that looked out over the raceway, "That pool look inviting to you, Clarence?"

When we sat down, David was wagging his head, muttering to himself, "Not safe. Not safe. Not safe. Not safe."

Jake hailed the waitress for a Bud; he sprinkled salt into
his palm and dumped it into the neck of the bottle. The rest
of us ordered iced tea, and we all had the special: fried fish,
French fries, and coleslaw. While we were waiting for blueberry pie, Jake chatted with Harry, two tables over, swap-
ping stories about the heat and discussing how the lobster
fishing was heading into its peak season. Ben was quiet all
through dinner. I thought maybe he was uncomfortable
with so many people around. He looked only at his plate,
and kept his wrist in his lap.

He did answer Sue's hello when she came over to our
table, but he quickly went back to concentrating on his
food. Sue and I talked over his head, and I invited her to
join us. "I'm getting mine to go," she said. "I have some
paperwork to get caught up on—insurance claims, patients'
files, that kind of thing. But, hey, don't you owe me a fishing date?"

We made sketchy plans to go out for mackerel some
time in the near future. A waitress at the front counter
called that her meal was ready, so Sue said good-bye, and
left to pick up the styrofoam package. Jake had another beer
and by the time we walked out of the restaurant, dusk was
falling and the air had cooled down a little. With a gleam in
his eye, David said, "I fool Marfa again," and headed for
the bridge.

"Oh no, you don't," I scolded, running around in front
of David, facing him with my hands on my hips. "What did
I say about that railing?"

"It not safe."

"That's right, and don't you forget it. Now, let's get on
home." I hooked my arm in his and turned him toward the

truck. Jake hooked David's other arm, and the three of us crossed the street.

"Swing me, Papa," David pleaded, remembering how we used to walk with him between us, lifting him off the ground, walking a few more steps, lifting him again.

Jake chuckled. "You're too big for swinging."

Ben was standing on the other side of the street, watching us, his hands shoved deep into the pockets of his cut-off jeans. "Come on, Ben," I called. "We're ready to leave."

"My Bennybuddy, go truck," David yelled as he climbed into the back.

Ben didn't move.

Jake called, "Get over here and drive for me. That last beer near put me to sleep. You don't want me nodding off at the wheel, do you?" Jake walked around to the passenger side as he took the keys out of his pocket. He held them over his head and jangled them.

At that, Ben started to move across the street toward us. Jake tossed him the keys, and they tinkled as they flew through the air. Ben reached up and caught the keys with one hand, the glow of the streetlight exposing the ugly mark on his wrist.

Pulling down the tailgate, I climbed into the truck bed with David. "Aren't we lucky?" I said to him. "We've got the coolest spot for riding."

"I hot." David wiped the moisture from under his neck.

Jake and Ben sat in the cab, and I could hear their muffled words through the open window. Jake was making wide sweeps with his hands as he talked. Ben kept his hands on the steering wheel but nodded his head often, and a few times he laughed. Grinding a cigarette into the overflowing ashtray on the dashboard, Jake talked about *The Sandpiper*, the twenty-eight foot boat he'd inherited from our father. He told Ben how he'd fished with that boat for a lot of years while he saved to trade up for *The Sybil*. I heard him say he'd helped Junior Turner at Turner Boatyard build the new boat, and they'd designed it so the hull was wider and the keel deeper than most. *The Sybil*, he bragged, was the most stable lobster craft that fished off Quarry Island.

Sitting in the truck bed, listening to Jake as he talked to Ben, I felt a tug on my sleeve. David was holding a small shiny object, which he tossed clumsily from hand to hand. Then, with a wide grin, he held both hands out to me, curled facedown into fists. "Guess, Marfa," he prodded. I could easily see which hand held the treasure; headlights from the car behind us glinted off the shiny object that was only half-concealed in the crook of his thumb and fingers.

I pretended to have a hard time deciding. "Um, let me think. It's in this hand. No, wait. I bet it's here, this one."

David grinned. "Nope." He uncurled his right fist and showed me a bronze nut-and-bolt lying in the sweaty creases of his palm.

"Is that Papa's?"

"Yep," he grinned.

The car behind turned into a lane and left us in the dark. We'd long since passed the village and were driving up Granite Road along the west end of the island. The houses were few and far between, and the only light was the soft glow of the bulb inside the cab. I pointed out fireflies to David, or "buglights" as he called them, until he fell asleep, leaning against the cab of the truck, clutching tightly his little bronze treasure.

When we reached Seal Point, Ben turned onto the sandy drive to my cottage. I gently poked David's thigh. "Wake up, sweetie," I whispered. His head bounced against the cab as the truck came to a stop, but he didn't wake. I pulled his head onto my shoulder. When Jake jumped out of the cab and came around back, I said, "We've got a sleepy boy here."

"So I see," Jake said as he unlatched the tailgate. He leaned into the truck bed and held his hand out for me.

I took Jake's hand but didn't move. "Let him stay the night with me. And all of tomorrow. David and I haven't had a day just to ourselves all summer."

Jake dropped my hand, and it seemed he was avoiding my eyes. "I don't know. He's been kinda skittery—maybe I should keep him with me. Besides, I'll need him in the morning to fill bait bags."

"Ben can help you with that."

Jake patted the pack of cigarettes in his shirt pocket and seemed to be weighing my request. Finally he said, "Well, guess it'd be all right," then he climbed into the truck bed and pulled his sleeping son to his feet. David woke long enough to be helped down out of the truck and up the stairs to the sun porch, then he slumped onto the daybed and fell back to sleep. While Jake pulled off David's brown work shoes and socks, I fluffed the feather pillow under his head and folded the wool army blanket at his feet. Though it had cooled down some, it was still a muggy night and he wouldn't need covers, even sleeping on the porch.

As I watched Jake pull out of the yard, I stood by the screen door, listening to David's snoring. Jake's headlights beamed onto the lane, illuminating branches of spruce and birch that hung over my sandy driveway. Then the yellow rays grew smaller, and the purr of the engine drifted off into the night as he turned south onto Granite Road and headed back toward Old Cove.

"I feel strange using David's bed when he's here," Ben said behind me.

"I don't believe we can move him," I said, latching the

screen door and flicking off the outside light.

Ben's face creased with worry. "I don't want David, you know, to feel like I'm pushing him out of his room."

"David's let other people use his room and has slept out here on the daybed, like when Grace and I entertained Boston friends here. He won't mind."

But I was wrong about that.

When I woke in the morning, the heat had not broken. It seemed we were in for another sweltering, muggy day. In the kitchen, I was measuring coffee for the pot when I glanced out the window and noticed Ben's bike was gone from its usual place against the shed. He must have ridden over to Old Cove to go out on *The Sybil* with Jake.

And David must have watched Ben leave. He sat on the edge of the daybed, clutching his little treasure from the night before. His shoulders were slack, and he stared at his wide, boxy feet planted on the porch floor.

"Want breakfast? You can fix yourself some cereal," I told him as I stood in the doorway, my hand on the jamb, the smell of coffee drifting over my shoulder.

David shifted heavily and slouched even more. His hands were clasped between his legs, gripping the bronze bolt. Without looking up, he shook his head vigorously from side to side.

"Not hungry?" I asked, coming onto the porch and standing in front of him. He continued to shake his head in that exaggerated way.

"Oh, I don't believe that. I've never known you to not be hungry," I teased him. Reaching under David's arms, I tried to lift him from the daybed. When I couldn't budge him, I gave up trying and instead stood in front of him and rubbed his pudgy shoulders through his T-shirt. Smoothing the thin strands of his hair, I leaned into him and pressed his face against the cool fabric of my robe.

My poor wounded boy, I thought.

I kissed the top of David's head, and he gave me a bear hug. "My poor baby," I murmured, stroking his cheek.

"I not baby, Marfa," he said. "I big man."

"That's right. David's a big man now." I swayed, rocking him. When David was sad like this, Grace would sing to him. So now I tried singing in my off-key voice. "Ring around the mulberry bush, the mulberry bush, the mulberry bush . . ." David began tapping his toes, slapping them against the plank floor.

When I finished, he pleaded, "Sing 'nother."

So I sang *Three Blind Mice*, then his favorite childhood song, the one Grace had made up for him: *10 Lobsters in a Trap*.

As I ended the song, way off tune, David raised his eyes. "Where Gracie at?" he asked.

At first, I couldn't answer; my eyes welled up and my voice choked. But when he asked again "Where Gracie at?" I forced myself to say, "Grace isn't here, remember?"

"Her go?"

"Yes," I said. "Gracie's gone."

At the kitchen table, I sipped a cup of coffee as David finished a bowl of Cheerios. He spooned out the last round O, then lifted the bowl to his lips and slurped the sweetened milk. After he wiped his mouth with the back of his hand, he got up from the chair and carried his bowl and spoon to the sink. He leaned over the sink and rinsed out his dishes, sweat marking the back of his shirt, a red bandanna sticking out of his pocket. He was still barefoot, the legs of his green work pants rolled up unevenly around his ankles.

I went over to him and wrapped my arms around his back; he smelled of rank sweat. Wiggling out of my embrace, David turned to face me, a quizzical look in his muddy eyes. I chucked his chin gently with my knuckles and said, "Ready to wash up and shave?"

David shook his head as he moved sideways like a crab, his back rubbing along the edge of the counter.

He made me laugh. "You're not trying to get out of cleaning up, are you?" I asked, putting my hands on my hips and tilting my head.

"I go work, Marfa. Help Cap'n Papa boat." He'd backed himself into a corner where the counter angled, and he leaned heavily against the edge of it, supporting himself with both hands.

"You've got a day off! Captain Papa gave you a vacation. What would you like to do today?"

"I stay you?"

"That's right. We'll spend the whole day together, just you and me. You can help me weed the flowerbed, maybe we'll take some pictures, might make a cake if it cools off. We could go to Lincoln Quarry for a swim. And you can help me fix supper for Ben and Papa when they get back. It's Saturday night, so that means beans and hot dogs, don't you think? We'll probably have to go into town and pick up some red hot dogs at the market. Okay?"

David nodded, his eyes lighting up.

"You sit here and make a picture while I take my shower." I got out a pad of paper and set it on the table. David sat down, and I handed him a box of Crayolas. "I'll be back in a few minutes. You draw a surprise for me, okay?"

A little later I came out of the bathroom, tying my robe around the waist and drying my hair with a towel. I said, "Now, let's see what you've drawn."

David's picture was of three circles, one on top of the other. The top circle had two dots for eyes and a line for a mouth. The bottom circle had two stick legs jutting out. But the middle circle was blank.

"Is it a boy?" I asked.

"Yep, boy." David started coloring the top circle red.

"Sure, I see. There's his head. That's what you're coloring now, right?"

"Yep, boy head." David switched to a blue crayon and began to color the bottom circle.

"And that's the lower part of the body," I said, leaning over David's back. His hair smelled sweaty. "You've drawn his legs, too. That's good."

David handed the picture to me. "I like your boy," I said. "But you forgot the arms. And the hands." Spreading the paper on the table, I pointed with a black crayon to the sides of the middle circle. "Why don't you add some arms and hands right here?"

David grabbed the black crayon from me and threw it down on the table. It broke into chunks. "Annh annh annh!" he moaned, pounding the table. The pieces of crayon danced and his drawing fluttered and slipped to the linoleum floor.

I stooped to pick it up. "Why, David? Why can't the boy have hands?"

He squeezed his eyes shut and shook his head vigorously.

"Well, it's a fine picture just the way it is. I tell you what. It's so hot and humid this morning, what if we go for a swim at the quarry?"

David stood up and leaned toward me. "Swim?" he asked, his face close to mine. "Today?"

"Yes. That'll be a good way to begin the day. I'll bet there's a pair of trunks in the dresser in your room."

"Ben room?"

"Well, your room too. But it's nice of you to share it with Ben. Come on, let's find those trunks."

I hadn't been in the small bedroom off the kitchen since Ben had moved in. It felt odd to be opening the door, even in my own house. As I went into the room, I noticed that Ben had not removed any of David's things; he'd stacked his own clothes on the floor of the closet or hung them on wire hangers.

David burst into the bedroom, dropping his drawing and the box of Crayolas on the bed. Then he pulled open all the drawers of his narrow blue dresser and pawed through his old favorites. From the top drawer he pulled out a worn baseball glove—the webbing on it ripped—a red Matchbox car, a half deck of cards. Then, from the second drawer he yanked out two pairs of athletic socks, a T-shirt Grace and I had bought him at the Rockland Lobster Festival, and a pair of pajamas.

"Can't find your swimsuit? Try the bottom drawer," I said. "Put those things back first." I helped him pick up the toys and clothes from the floor and bed where he'd tossed them. In the last drawer, he found the old pair of tan boxer trunks, a pair of goggles, and his Mickey Mouse beach towel. "Good," I said. "I'll close the door and give you your privacy while you get your suit on. I'll put my bathing suit on, too, then we'll be ready to go over to the quarry."

In my own bedroom, I changed into a reliable old navy blue Jantzen, then slipped a blouse and a pair of shorts on over it. From the bathroom I grabbed a faded yellow beach towel.

While waiting in the kitchen for David, I fixed a thermos of lemonade and rinsed out the few breakfast dishes. David still hadn't come out of his room. Finally, I knocked on the door, but he didn't answer. I swung it open. David was sitting on the edge of the bed holding Ben's red notebook and scribbling in it with a purple crayon. He liked to pretend to write, but he could only make a few letters, so he had scrawled a full page of crooked *D*'s, *M*'s and *3*'s.

I snatched the notebook away from him. "David! That's not yours!" He looked up at me, confused. After all, this was his room and in the past everything in it had been for him to use.

I held the journal tightly and took a deep breath, while David snapped the crayon in half and peeled off the paper sleeve. "All right," I said, "we can't do anything about it now. We'll just have to explain to Ben, that's all." I flipped through the pages, glad to discover he had marked only the back of the last page Ben had written on. As I was ready to close the notebook, I noticed that David's scribbling followed several new entries.

David was chewing a crayon stub, and his teeth were covered with purple wax. I wrenched his hand away from his mouth and pried the crayon from him, tossing it into a wastebasket next to the maple desk. Then I set Ben's notebook on the desk and pulled David to his feet. "Go brush your teeth so we can go swimming."

He lumbered into the bathroom and found his toothbrush in the little rack that also held mine. He brushed hard, spat, and raised his head from the sink. While he watched himself in the mirror, he said, "My teef clean. I go swim." Smiling widely, he admired his teeth.

I stepped into the bathroom, lifted a hand towel from the rack, and wiped the froth of toothpaste from the corners of his mouth. "Just one more thing." I opened the medicine cabinet to get a disposable razor. "Let's get rid of those whiskers."

"White stuff on face?" he asked, taking down a can of shaving cream from the medicine cabinet.

"Yes. You can spread that on your face. Shake it well first."

David shut the cabinet so he could watch himself again in the mirror. He peered closely as he rubbed foam on his cheeks and chin. Then he sat on the closed toilet lid and let me shave him. When David was at Jake's house he was able to shave himself using an electric razor, but I was afraid he'd slip and get cut with a straight edge. He stayed patient as long as I let him hold a hand mirror to look at himself while I scraped away foam and skimpy bristles from his face.

I patted his cheeks with the towel. After David examined himself, I took the hand mirror from him and set it on a shelf under the sink. "There, don't you look handsome! Maybe when we get back from swimming, I'll trim your hair, too."

But David was already out of the bathroom and into the kitchen. He grabbed his goggles and slung the Mickey Mouse towel around his neck. "Go swim now, Marfa."

"Okay, I guess you earned it. Wait, what've you got there?" Something shiny stuck out of the small flap pocket of his trunks.

David covered the pocket with his hand. "Mine," he said, planting his feet squarely on the gray linoleum.

"Let me see." I pushed his hand aside, reached into the pocket, and found a gold penlight. "This is Ben's! You can't go taking other people's things, David. Now, go put it back where you found it in Ben's room."

"David room."

"Well, yes. But Ben's using it right now, and that penlight belongs to him." I gave his shoulders a light push. "Put it back if you want to go swimming."

Reluctantly, he shuffled into the bedroom, and I heard the penlight clunk as he dropped it onto the desk.

At Lincoln Quarry, I parked in the gravel turnaround. David was out of the car before I could get the key free of the ignition. "Wait up," I called as he headed for the edge of the quarry. He stopped in his tracks and waited for me. I hastily grabbed my towel from the back seat and caught up with him. "Good boy," I said, laying my arm over his shoulders. We walked together to the shallowest end of the quarry. A group of loud teenagers were swimming and sunbathing at the other end.

Grace and I had liked to swim in saltwater, sometimes going down to our cove when the days got hot, but the icy coldness and strong undertow of the ocean frightened David. So we'd always brought him to Lincoln Quarry, even though it was not a friendly swimming hole. The quarry had been excavated a century earlier by men and oxen hauling out huge slabs of granite to be used all over the east coast in buildings, bridges, and monuments. It was now a deep jagged bowl of dark water. An orange life preserver hung on a nail near where we would swim, and there were posted signs that read *No Food or Pets* and *Swim At Your Own Risk*.

I shed my blouse, shorts, and deck shoes and set them on a boulder, and David dropped his towel beside them. After he fitted his plastic goggles over his eyes, he announced, "I ready."

"Let's do it, then. I'll go first. Don't go in until I tell you to. Okay?"

"Yep." Excitedly, he danced from foot to foot.

"Wait right there until I tell you it's okay," I warned. At the shallow end, I climbed down the granite wall where it was cut away and made a kind of stairway. Stepping into the deliciously cold water, which was up to my waistline, I walked out on a rock shelf. "Okay, David," I yelled. "You can come in now."

He walked gingerly down the sloped wall, but as he neared the bottom he belly-flopped into the water, sending a spray onto my face and arms. Struggling to find his footing and to stand upright, he sputtered water from his mouth. David was not much of a swimmer, but he knew how to hold his breath under water, how to tread water, and how to dog paddle. He'd never learned any more advanced strokes, such as the crawl or the sidestroke, and he could only float for a short time before he sank like a dead weight.

Sybil used to worry about him when he went out on the boat and always insisted he wear a floatation belt. But Jake usually let him take it off as soon as they got out of Old Cove and out of sight. The belt got in the way while David filled bait bags.

David found his footing and slammed his palms on the surface, directing a splash at me.

"Hey, watch it!" I laughed. "None of that rough stuff."

We swam and played in the water, and came out, climbing up the cut-away granite wall to the top edge of the quarry. I slipped my clothes over my wet suit. David was grinning as he dried himself with his beach towel.

"Put that on the seat under you," I reminded him as he headed for the car.

"Yep." Happily, he spread the towel over the passenger seat and patted it into place.

I took a thermos from the trunk and filled two paper cups. The sun shone hotly and a monarch butterfly flitted around us as David and I sat on a blanket and sipped lemonade. When I leaned toward him to refill his paper cup, he threw his arms around my neck and hugged me so tightly he almost cut off my breath. He planted a slobbery kiss on my cheek and giggled, "I luf you, Marfa."

That afternoon, we worked in the garden. Kneeling near a bed of lupine, David weeded around the purple flowers. A monarch butterfly circled his back, but he was unaware of it as he moved on to deadhead the pansies. He seemed to have a special sense when it came to working with plants and didn't need much supervision. I left him to clean up a patch of Shasta daisies while I caught a quick catnap in the hammock. When I woke, it was to the smell of phlox and Sweet William. David thrust a bouquet under my nose. With a sleepy smile, I took the flowers from his grasp. "David, these are lovely. Thank you."

"Put in water, Marfa."

"Yes. That's a good idea. Let's give them something to drink." I slid out of the hammock and followed him into the cottage. We filled a vase and set the flowers on the wicker stand on the sun porch.

While we were on the sun porch, I trimmed David's hair, with him watching in the hand mirror while I snipped. As I was putting the final touches on his haircut, Jake's pick-up pulled into the yard. David pushed my hand aside and ran outdoors, the screen door banging behind him. Rushing up to the truck as it pulled to a stop, he called, "I go swim, Papa!"

Jake reached out of the open side window and tousled his hair, "You did, did you?"

"And David helped me in the garden," I said, coming up behind him. "He gathered a nice bouquet of flowers."

"Pick flowers," David bragged, beaming as he walked around the front of the truck and climbed into the passenger side.

Resting my hip against the driver's door, I said, "David weeded for me. I haven't kept up with the gardens like Grace would have."

"Big mess," David said earnestly, bouncing on the truck seat.

Jake chuckled. "Ayuh, he can be a help when he puts his mind to it." But then a frown darkened his face, and he leaned toward the window. "So it went okay?" he asked. "David behaved himself for you?"

"Of course," I answered. "Why wouldn't he?" Jake didn't say anything, but a look of relief flickered across his face as he waved and pulled out of the driveway.

After they left, I swept up the sun porch and carried the dustpan out to the pinewoods behind the cottage, where I spread David's hair for the birds to use in their nests.

CHAPTER 10

On a Saturday, I had a strange conversation with Ben. Around suppertime, he rode his bike back from painting at the Tuttle's, carrying a paper bag over the handlebars. He seemed moody, barely said hello, grunted when I asked how his day had been. After he washed up, he handed me an Italian sandwich he'd bought in the village. Instead of sitting down with me at the table, he took his own sandwich outside and sat in one of the Adirondack chairs in front of the cottage.

I didn't mind eating my sandwich alone at the kitchen table; there was no need to make conversation and no one to mind if I read *The Island News*. After supper, I cleared off the table and got out my camera bag. Removing the lens, I used a blower brush to clean inside the body. With lens cleaning fluid and paper, I wiped the viewfinder, then cleaned the lens before replacing it.

A couple of hours passed, and still Ben hadn't budged from the chair. Whenever I glanced out the window, he was sitting in the same position, his elbow on the wide arm of the chair, his chin in his hand. Finally, I went out to check on him. With his thumb, he was rubbing the mole over his eyebrow and seemed deep in thought.

"Anything bothering you?" I asked.

He refused to look up at me. "Un unh."

"Oh, come now," I said, sitting down in the chair next to him. "If something's bugging you, tell me."

"It's not important." He stared out at the sea, fingering that mole, a dark look on his face.

"All right. If you don't want to talk, that's your choice," I said, starting to get up.

"I heard some things," he said, still not looking at me, his neck flushing.

"What kind of things?" I asked, dropping back into the chair.

"Stuff the guys down at the co-op were saying."

Now what? "Well, what'd they say?"

"Something about you and Grace."

"Oh? Like . . . ?"

"Just stuff. But it got me to wondering, you know, where did Grace sleep?"

"You mean here? When we were at the cottage?"

"Yeah. I'm using David's room. There's only one other bedroom, and that's yours."

What a naive kid! Did I have to spell it out for him? I thought he'd figured all this out long before now. I certainly hadn't kept my love for Grace a secret. "Grace slept in my room, with me."

"But in Boston, in your apartment, she had her own room?"

"No, don't be silly. We always shared a bedroom, no matter where we were."

He gazed blankly at the red sun going down over the ocean.

"Ben, look at me." He turned slowly toward me, but his eyes shifted to the ground. "Grace and I always slept in the same bed. You understand what that means?"

His face flushed. "What the guys were saying is true?"

I folded my hands in my lap. "If they said I loved her, then yes, that's damn right. Grace and I were a couple. You don't have a problem with that, do you?"

"What's Jake think about it?"

"We didn't tell him at first. But that was years ago, when Grace first started coming here with me. We let him think we were just friends. Then one day I got mad at him when he called the harbormaster a pansy-ass queer. I told him to quit talking that way because I was queer too."

Ben flinched at *queer*. "What did Jake say?"

"Oh, something like, 'The fellows on the dock have been saying I got a dyke for a sister.' And I said right back at him, 'You do.'"

Ben seemed to jump on this. "So, Jake didn't think it was right for you and Grace to be . . . like that?"

"You mean lesbians?" Again he winced at my words. "To tell you the truth, I don't know. I never really cared; it wasn't going to change the way I felt about Grace. After a while, Jake just got used to Grace and me being together. She was like another sister to him."

Ben's jaw tightened as he said, "There was a gay man in our fellowship a few years ago, and my father said he needed to be freed from a lustful homosexual spirit. He prayed over him, but the man wouldn't repent. So the church excommunicated him."

"Do you think that was the best thing for your church to do?"

"My father says homosexuality is ungodly."

"For crying out loud!" I snorted. "You don't think Pastor Ralph is the expert on God?"

"Well no, but the whole church . . ." Ben mumbled.

I was pissed now. "I'll tell you one thing, Ben. There's nothing the least bit evil about what Grace and I felt for each other. I can't believe loving someone is a sin."

Ben didn't argue, he just sat thinking and staring at the sea. After a while, he stood up and went inside to bed without saying goodnight.

Sunday began badly. I was awakened by thunder that seemed to begin at one end of the sky and rumble across to the other. It hadn't started to rain, but lightning flashed like a flickering fluorescent bulb. When the rain finally came, I thought *good*, maybe it'll cool things down. The drops fell slowly at first, and then harder and harder until there was a steady pelting.

Because of the thunder, I hardly heard the knock at my bedroom door. But then it got louder.

"Yes?" I called out, swinging my legs over the side of the bed.

"I want to talk to you." Ben's voice shot through the door.

"All right. Just a minute." I quickly threw on some clothes, then stepped into the hallway, closing my bedroom door behind me. I didn't want Ben staring at the photos of Grace that wall-papered my room.

Ben was holding his red notebook, which shook in his hand. As he tried to say something, he stammered, then he turned abruptly and strode down the hallway toward the kitchen. I followed him.

Ben sat down, dropping into a ladderback chair and slamming his notebook onto the kitchen table.

As I passed the open door to his bedroom, I glanced in and noticed that the top drawer of the desk was open.

David's crayons were spilled all over. The storm outside had picked up speed and so I crossed the kitchen, the linoleum sticking to my bare feet, and closed the window.

Ben glared at me and jabbed at the notebook with his index finger. "You've been reading this again."

"Wait a minute. You're wrong about that . . ."

He didn't let me finish. Jumping up from the table, he nearly knocked over his chair. Its legs rattled on the linoleum. "What's this then? All this damn scribbling all over the place? What'd you do, read it and then let David use it as a coloring book?" He pointed to the notebook on the table.

Rain was pinging through the screens and dripping onto the plank floor of the sun porch, so I shut the door between the porch and the kitchen.

Ben's face was flushed, with red spots high on his cheeks, as he sputtered, "I should've known better than to trust you! I'm such a fucking fool—should've learned by now not to trust *anyone*. Why are you snooping in my things again?"

"I didn't do it," I said with my hands on my hips. "Don't go jumping to conclusions. It's not at all what you think."

"Oh yeah? Sure looks like it to me. Like you've been nosing around in my private stuff again."

"I didn't . . ."

"To hell you didn't." He picked up the notebook and it fell open in his hands. David's purple letters were like scars across the page. "How'd this happen?" The notebook trembled in his hand.

I made a small laugh. "David was just trying to be like you. Pretending to write, filling up the page with letters. I didn't even know he had it."

Ben flung the notebook across the room. It skittered on the linoleum, stopping half-in, half-out of his bedroom door. "Yeah, sure. How did he get my journal? I left it in the desk. Thought it'd be fucking safe there."

"It is! I didn't read any of your new entries."

Ben's eyes widened. "Yeah? Then how do you know I've been writing in it again?"

I sat down heavily. Everything seemed so complicated. What had I gotten myself into? "You don't understand."

"That's for damn sure."

"David did it. He was in your room—*his* room, really—to get his swimsuit, and he found his crayons and your notebook . . ." My voice trailed off. I couldn't muster the energy to explain, and Ben's anger seemed inflated, out of proportion. "I guess the rest is history, isn't it?"

"Damn right. And so am I. I'm out of here. Today." Stamping across the kitchen, Ben stooped to pick up the notebook. He slammed his bedroom door behind him, but it sprung open again. He pulled shirts and jeans off hangers, scooped dirty socks and underwear from the closet floor, grabbed the gold penlight from the desk, stuffing everything into his gray gym bag.

He came out of the bedroom, his gym bag slung over his shoulder, strode past me, and flung open the door to the porch. The screen door banged. I watched out the window as he got on his bicycle. Ben hung the bag over his neck like a backpack and rode off in the rain.

Well, damn him anyway! Here I'd given up a good part of my summer to help him—and this was how he showed his gratitude. I was going to make sure he'd left nothing of his behind. If he had, I would send it right over to him. Including his damn ring. I'd get rid of all his stuff. Reclaim my own space.

I found a pair of his socks and a Tom Clancy paperback, which I packed up. But I couldn't find the ring. It wasn't in my top dresser drawer, where I thought I'd left it. I checked the pockets of the shorts I'd worn the night we all went to the Seagull's Nest. Except for a tissue and two aspirin, they were empty. I rummaged through the other drawers of my dresser, the closet, the bedside table. On my hands and knees, I looked under the bed and in the corners of my bedroom. I hunted in every room in the cottage and on the sun porch.

When I searched the darkroom, I discovered that the photo of the ring had disappeared too. Strange. I'd been in the darkroom the day before, mounting some of the prints for the art show, and saw the ring photo lying on the worktable. It wasn't there now. I stooped down to see if the photograph had fallen to the floor. Shredded pieces of paper were scattered under the workbench. Picking them up, I spread them on the worktable and fit them together like a jigsaw puzzle. It was the photo of the ring, all right. Had Ben discovered it and ripped it up? What else was in store for me concerning that kid? I wasn't in the mood to deal with anything having to do with Ben. Leaving the pieced-together picture on the workbench, I closed the darkroom.

It seemed good to have the cottage to myself again. I walked around without a robe on, left the bathroom door open when I was in there, fixed meals for only one person whenever it suited me. I got up in the morning when I wanted to, went to bed when I wanted. My CD's of women's music got a good workout—Chris Williamson, Kay Gardner, Ferron—all the music I hadn't played while Ben was with me.

But as the days went by, I began to miss him. Not that I wanted him living with me again, but I did wonder how he was doing. You're like a damn mother hen, I scolded myself. Whenever I'd start worrying about him, I'd tell myself, 'Let the kid go. He got by for 18 years without you, he can do it just fine again.'

I knew Ben was living at the Tuttle house. Jake had told me he was still hauling traps with him in the morning and painting the clapboards and trim in the afternoons.

One afternoon when I was at Parson's Grocery, picking up a few things, I overheard Julia Whiting tell Harry that Owen and Emily Tuttle were happy with their retirement in Florida. She said it was for sure, they were putting the Maine house up for sale—her niece who worked at Quarry Island Realty told her they'd already signed a contract. As I eavesdropped, digging into my wallet for change, I realized Ben would need to finish the paint job soon.

As I was driving home along Granite Road, I met Jake's truck headed toward town. We both slowed to a stop, pulling up next to each other. Jake stuck his head out the window to ask me about Ben. "That boy's always a quiet one. But nowadays I can't get more than two words outta him," he told me. "Something's bothering him, you better believe. He's carrying some awful load on his shoulders."

"There was trouble between him and his father," I explained. "They had a falling out."

"That so? What brought that on?'"

"I think Ben should tell you himself when he's ready."

Jake pressed for more information. "How come he's gone back to Tuttle's and ain't staying at your place anymore?"

"For crying out loud, Jake, I didn't take him in for good. Ben's a big boy, he can manage on his own. He's got to get that painting finished, and it's a lot easier for him if he's right there."

"But that's all there is to it? Feels to me like there's something sour between the two of you."

"Well, he heard some gossip at the co-op and found out I'm gay. Though, I can't imagine that he hadn't already figured that out. Anyway, it bothers him, I guess. Which is his problem, not mine. And he got this crazy notion that I was prying into his private stuff. Which I wasn't."

Jake shrugged his shoulders, but I could tell he was still concerned. "Look," I said, "if you're worried about him, have him go talk to Sue. She'll know better than any of us what to do."

A construction truck honked behind Jake. He waved out his window at the driver and said to me just before he pulled away, "I don't think Ben's gonna talk to anyone."

As I continued along home, I had to admit to myself that I was worried about Ben too.

A few days later, I phoned Sue, but she said she hadn't heard a word from Ben. Before she hung up, she reminded me of my promise to go fishing with her.

That evening, she showed up at my cottage. We walked the path down to the little boathouse at the edge of the cove. My 16-foot wooden boat, though small, was heavy and awkward, but we managed to push it on its skids into the sea. It was the same boat I'd had since I was a girl; it was wide and stable and I loved puttering around in it. The inside slats were painted gray, and the wooden hull was dark green. Grace and I had always enjoyed using the boat to fish for mackerel, though neither of us liked the oily taste of that particular fish. Every summer, we caught a number of them, especially when they were running, and we always could find someone to give our catch to.

Sue and I set out in the boat, with her sitting near the bow and me at the helm. I pulled on the rope of the fifty-horse motor several times until it kicked in. We didn't venture beyond the head of the cove, but trolled close to shore.

For a while, we fished in silence, enjoying the comfortable companionship of old friends, the peaceful bobbing of the boat, and the lulling pulse of the motor. Then Sue asked about Ben. "He's not living with you anymore?"

"He left in kind of a huff."

"What happened?"

"You won't believe this. It took him all this time to figure out I'm gay, and he's having a hard time with it."

"Hel-*lo*! It's the new millennium! What's the big deal? So you're gay, so what?" Sue said.

A puddle of water and motor oil sloshed in the bottom of the boat, making oily rainbows that swirled under the slats. I picked a lure out of the puddle and set it back into the tackle box. "It's his father's influence, " I said. "All his life he's heard that crap about homosexuality being a sin. You know how that story goes."

"Sure do," Sue said as she let out a little more line. "It'll be hard for him to shake those kinds of messages."

I turned the tiller to follow the shoreline. "I think it's more than that," I said, then went on to tell her that Ben thought I'd been reading his notebook again.

"Maybe the prying was the reason."

"Who knows?"

"On the other hand, maybe it was just an excuse for him to latch onto. Someone like Ben, who's never known a healthy relationship, must be terrified of intimacy." Sue took off her visor, wiped sweat from her brow, shook her frizzy hair, and set the visor back on her head. "He probably sees you as a parental figure—which brings up all the unresolved issues with his own folks."

I watched a pair of porpoises making surface dives.

"What really worries me," I said, "is that Ben might do something to himself again."

"You can't stop him if he really wants to, Martha. No one can. What you've given him these last few weeks—by showing him that someone cares about him—is all you can do. And that's a lot." Sue trailed her fingers in the water, making little ripples. "I think the rest is up to him. If he starts hurting badly enough, maybe he'll come talk with me, or go over to Pen Bay and see Doctor Turner."

"But what if he doesn't ask for help, even when he needs it?"

"Look, if you're really that concerned, I'll stop by some afternoon soon and talk with Ben. Check on how he's doing, see if his Zoloft is running out. The salesman was at my office just last week and left some samples. Ben can have those if he's still low on money." Sue added, "He's back at the Tuttle house?"

"Um hum. He goes out lobstering with Jake in the mornings, but I imagine he's usually home by late afternoon."

"That's a good sign if he's still fishing with Jake."

"I suppose it is. Anyway, I really would feel better if you'd talk to Ben," I said.

Suddenly I felt a hard tug on my line and my pole bent toward the water. Setting the hook, I began reeling, making sure to keep the tip of my pole in the air. Mackerel are a stiff fish, and I could feel the pull as the fish fought the line, but there was not a lot of play, just the steady work of reeling. Once the fish broke the surface, Sue scooped with the net. The silvery-black mackerel flopped around the floor of the boat, so I tossed it into a Styrofoam cooler and replaced the cover. As I cast again, throwing my line out over the water, I could hear the fish thrashing about, trying to break free.

When we got back to the cottage, Jake's truck was

parked in the yard. He was sitting outside in one of the Adirondack chairs, drinking a beer. Sue and I showed him our catch.

"Not bad," he said.

"Good," I told him. "You can take them home with you for supper."

"Not till you clean 'em first."

"I always clean my own fish, you know that."

Jake and Sue chatted, while I went inside. I gutted the five mackerel in the kitchen sink, slitting the bellies, pulling out the entrails. As I worked, David wandered throughout the cottage. He finally settled on the living room floor, where he clumsily shuffled an old deck of playing cards and stacked them in little piles, muttering, "Deal. Deal."

I hadn't noticed when I went to bed, but first thing in the morning I realized that Grace's gold chain was missing. It had been draped over the rosewood box on my dresser all summer. Where in the world could it have gone?

Damn! Things were always disappearing around here. Good lord, had David taken Grace's chain again? It seemed likely that he might have pocketed it when he was here last night.

I drove over to Old Cove and turned into Jake's driveway. *The Sybil* was not on its mooring, meaning that Jake, David and Ben were out hauling traps. As I walked toward the house, my eyes were drawn toward the cupola, that small room of windows on the roof.

At the front step, I tried the door. It opened easily. Jake never locked the door, and I let myself in as I had so many times over the years. I was familiar with every niche of this house where I'd grown up. Even the smell was familiar: the rubbery scent of foul-weather gear hung to dry, the acrid odor of tobacco, the overly sweet perfume of Jake's Old Spice.

I went directly to David's bedroom on the second floor. His room was a mess, as always: clothes strewn around on the floor, bed unmade, Tonka trucks and coloring books piled in the corner, a battered boombox and cassettes of country western music on the dresser.

While hanging David's washed clothes in his closet and stuffing the dirty ones into a laundry bag, I checked all his pockets for Grace's gold chain. The bronze nut-and-bolt was in a pair of work pants. Opening the dresser drawers, I sorted through David's underwear, making a mental note to mend some of his shorts and darn a few socks. Then I went through the pile of trucks and coloring books, where I found several silvery washers and a roofing nail. As I changed the sheets on his bed, I checked in the bedclothes and under the mattress. Finally, I swept the floor and cleaned out under the bed, tossing away a pair of mismatched slippers, but there was no sign of the gold chain.

I was ready to leave when I spotted a shoebox shoved onto the shelf in his closet. When I dumped the contents of it onto his bed, a couple of fishing lures, an old leather wallet, three cats-eye marbles, some felt pens without caps, and a mica rock tumbled out. Holding the box upside down, I shook it, but it was empty. I began to put his treasures back, but when I came to the wallet, I noticed how it bulged. Spreading it open, I reached into it. My fingers clutched something hard and round—Ben's ring. There were his initials *BG* and the engraving *Love No Other*. I slipped the ring into my pocket and dug deeper in the wallet. Sure enough. Grace's gold chain was scrunched up in the bottom crease. Damn David! I dug it out and fastened it around my neck.

The change pocket of the wallet still bulged. I unsnapped

it, expecting to find shiny pennies. But instead of coins, I saw Grace's pendant! The one with the pearl birthstone set into a gold heart. The one that had been missing from her gold chain when Jake brought her body into the dock last fall.

Feeling numb, I plopped down onto the bed. What did this mean? How in the world did David get Grace's pendant?

I stood clumsily. Clutching Grace's pendant in my hand, I walked with rubbery legs down the stairs, out the front door, and across the meadow. For a brief moment, I stopped and looked back at the house, my eyes drifting up toward the cupola, the glass room we called the Widow's Walk.

By now it was mid-afternoon, and *The Sybil* was visible in the harbor, tied up to the lobster car. Making my way down the gangway onto the floating wharf, I felt as if I were sleepwalking. I waited numbly as Jake finished storing his day's catch in an underwater crate. As he motored over to his mooring, he spotted me and waved. I didn't wave back.

Jake, David, and Ben climbed down from the larger boat into the skiff and rowed across the cove. When they reached the wharf, Ben seemed embarrassed to see me, but he threw a line and automatically I caught it and wrapped it around a cleat.

"Hi, Marfa," David called, waving from his seat in the skiff. I couldn't look at him.

"Send the boys someplace, Jake," I said. "I need to talk to you."

Jake appeared surprised at my abruptness and about ready to object. But he must have noticed the look on my face, because he said, "Ben, you and David take this oarlock into town and get a replacement. Take my truck. The keys are in it."

"I stay Papa." David sat stubbornly in the middle seat of the skiff.

"Go on, now. Do what Captain Papa says," Jake told him sternly.

As Ben stepped onto the wharf, he avoided looking at me. Motioning to David, he said, "Hey dude, what do you say we get an ice cream cone at the Seagull's Nest?" David climbed out of the boat and followed willingly to the truck. They drove out of Jake's driveway, headed toward Hailey's Harbor.

Jake tied off the dinghy and climbed onto the floating wharf. "What's this all about, sis?"

I thrust my left hand toward Jake. Grace's pearl-and-gold pendant danced in front of his eyes.

Jake's face blanched. "Where'd you find that?"

"In David's room. It's Grace's, isn't it? I want to know just how David got it."

Jake brushed past me and strode up the gangway. "Don't mean a thing," he tossed back at me.

I dashed after him, grabbing the tail flap of his flannel shirt. "How'd he get it, Jake?"

He stepped onto land. "Jesus, how would I know?"

"I bet you do know. There's something you're not telling me."

"Martha, this is a bunch of bullshit. You ain't making a bit of sense," Jake said he headed across the meadow.

I ran around in front of him. "Tell me! Why was this in David's room?"

Jake stiffened. "You don't know what you're asking. For Chrissakes, don't go putting your nose into this."

Grabbing my brother's shirtsleeve, I led him across the meadow toward the house. When we reached the granite step, I pulled him down and we sat side by side. "Jake," I said, holding tightly onto his hand, "there's a lot you and I don't talk about. But you've *never* kept anything important from me."

Jake wrenched free and lit a cigarette. His drags on it were deep, and he smoked intently, staring out at *The Sybil* where she sat on her mooring. Finally, grinding the cigarette butt with the heel of his boot, he muttered, "Sonofabitch, like I told you already, it was an accident."

"You mean Grace?" I sighed heavily, my fists clenched in my lap. "But that's not true, is it? It wasn't just an accident. Good God, Jake, I have to know what really happened." When he still wouldn't answer me, I threatened, "If you don't tell me, I'm going to ask David."

Jumping up from the granite slab, Jake stood looking down at me. "Don't bring David into this! He's just starting to forget about Grace and everything that happened out there that day."

"Then you tell me!" I yanked him back down beside me, grabbing his hands and squeezing them. I was ready to beg. "Please, Jake. I need to know what took place out there. What happened to Grace?"

He dropped his eyes and I felt a shudder run through him. "You probably figured it out already."

"Figured what out?"

"He did it," he mumbled.

"You mean David? David was responsible in some way?"

Jake nodded. Staring at the crushed cigarette butt at his feet he said, "He didn't mean to. Chrissakes, he loved her. You know that well as I do. David wouldn't hurt nobody on purpose, especially not Gracie."

"But he did, didn't he? What? He pushed her? Is that the way it happened?"

"He got upset, is all. Like he does sometimes. You know how he gets his mind fixed on something and can't let go of it."

I dropped Jake's hands. "Was it over the pendant?"

"The truth is, David got a liking for that thing. We was

just about done hauling. Gracie was standing by the port gunwale, I remember, telling some of them stories about her students. She sure enough could tell a story, couldn't she?" Jake looked at me then.

"Go on, Jake," I prodded. "Tell me all of it."

"Well, David saw that thing hanging around her neck and he just kept after her. Pestering her to look at it. I had to keep nagging him to get back to work on the bait barrel. But even when he was filling bags, he kept looking over his shoulder. At that damn necklace. Gracie was so patient, she was always so patient with David. Didn't get riled none. She held it out so's he could see it better. But then he started begging for it. Wanted it for hisself. You know how he can go on and on. Beat a thing to death. 'Me have it, Gracie,' he kept teasing. Finally both of us got damn frigging tired of him going on like that. I said, 'Quit it now, David.' Grace put the necklace inside her shirt, trying to hide it so he wouldn't think about it anymore."

"That wasn't the end of it, though, was it?"

"'Fraid not. We was about ready to come in, on the last string of pots, when David got kind of crazy. 'I have it,' he screamed. Over and over, going on like he does. Jesus, I had to set him down on the deck to get him to quiet down. Thought he was gonna be all right then, but quick as lightning he jumped up and reached for Gracie."

"He grabbed Grace?"

"Scared her. Clear as day I remember she said, 'Stop that, David. Be a good boy.' That's the last thing she ever said, 'Be a good boy, David.' I keep hearing those words, you know what I mean, just like she was standing here saying them now."

I could barely stand to listen.

"He got hold of her and yelled 'Mine!' Snatched at the necklace, real fast. It surprised Grace, I know it did cause her eyes got big. Jesus, I can still see her stepping back. She started to put her hands up to her neck, but then the boat ran into a swell and she . . . Grace's feet slid out from under her. I couldn't get to her in time. To this day I hear that cracking sound . . . her head slamming the washboard." Jake wiped his forehead roughly. "That's it. That's how it happened. Her neck got smacked by the coaming."

I didn't remember getting into my car or driving home. But later that night I found myself sitting on my screened porch. Out of the darkness floated the chirp of crickets, in the past a sound Grace and I had always loved, now a relentless whine I could hardly bear. All night I sat in the chair, too numb to even rock. My body felt limp and leaden at the same time. I sat with my arms folded tightly across my chest, barely aware of the shifting light: the darkness that settled on the bay, the clouds that moved all night, back and forth across the moon.

At dawn, when I finally tried to move, my back and shoulders were stiff. I tried to push myself up from the rocker, but I fell back into the seat. Dropping my head into my hands, I wept. I'd never before felt such helpless rage.

After a while, I got up and went inside the cottage. And I did something I'd never done before: I locked the door against my brother and his son.

CHAPTER 11

I should call Sue, I thought. Tell her what I'd found out about Grace's death. It would help to talk to someone. But, as angry as I was with Jake for lying to me, as furious as I was with David for making Grace fall, I worried about what might happen to David if anyone knew he was responsible for the accident. I didn't know if the authorities on the mainland would take him away. For manslaughter, maybe? What would they do with someone like David? Put him in one of those places, like the institution at Sprucehaven that Jake dreaded so much? I couldn't risk that happening. So I didn't tell anyone, not even Sue. I kept telling myself to do what Grace would want, and I could almost hear what she would say: *It wasn't really David's fault. He didn't know what he was doing. He didn't understand his own strength.*

And I felt something new. I was afraid of David now. What if David lost his temper again and hurt someone else? Could I keep quiet and take a chance that might happen?

I tossed around Jake's explanation about what had happened on the boat. "David didn't mean no harm," he'd said. That was probably true. David wouldn't hurt anyone on purpose. I kept seeing the desperation in my brother's eyes, so afraid he'd lose his son.

For two days, I didn't step out of the cottage. Jake kept phoning, but whenever I heard his voice I hung up. Finally, I took the phone off the hook. I couldn't do the simplest chores, like washing dishes or sweeping the floor. I forgot to eat, woke in the middle of the night, then couldn't fall back to sleep. Every time I closed my eyes, I saw Grace in her last moment: David grabbing at her, the startled, unbelieving expression on her face.

In the morning when I woke, the first thing I saw was the small rosewood box on the dresser and Grace's fishing hat hanging on the mirror. It seemed strange that Grace had not worn the hat the day she went out on *The Sybil* with Jake and David.

Grace had owned that hat for almost fifteen years. It was navy blue, but faded, the brim stained with Old Woodsman Fly Dope, the sweatband ringed. A few times I tried to convince her to wash it, but she insisted that the stains were part of its history.

Once, Grace even wore the hat to bed. Early in the season, shortly after we'd arrived at the cottage, I'd been outside picking lilacs. When I came into the bedroom with my arms full, Grace had just finished a bath and was standing nude, getting ready to dress. "Just the hat," I said. Grace looked at me like I was crazy, so I said again, "Put the hat on. Nothing else."

Grace squinted her green eyes at me. "What are you up to now?"

"Go ahead. Put it on," I insisted.

Grace took the hat down from the mirror's edge and turned it around in her hands. "I don't know what you have in mind. And I'm almost afraid to ask."

"Go on," I said again.

So Grace put the hat on, and stood in front of me in the early June sunlight. "Over there." I gestured with my head, nodding toward the bed. By then Grace had caught my playful mood and bounced onto the bed eagerly.

"Okay, now what?" Grace patted the bedspread.

"Lie down." Grace started to take off the hat, so I said, "Keep it on."

All this time my arms were full of lilacs. When Grace stretched out on the bed, I picked off tiny petal after petal, dropping them onto her freckled body. Grace smiled up at me as the blossoms blanketed her.

Lying on the bed beside Grace, I smelled the scent of lilac everywhere. The small purple petals clung to Grace's nipples, filled her navel, bedded down in her red pubic hair. I began to nibble them from her body, picking them off with my lips, sucking the sweet lilacs. Sucking her sweetness. I lay on top of Grace, the full length of her, and we ground the petals into perfume.

From that day, Grace took to wearing Eau de Lilac and whenever she put on the hat, she winked at me.

On the third morning, the phone was still off the hook so I wouldn't get Jake's calls. I didn't want to see him or talk to him. In my bedroom, I sat on the edge of the bed and looked through an album that contained pictures of David that I'd taken over the years. There he was at two-and-a-half, Jake crouched behind to make it look as if he were standing by himself. After I'd snapped that photo, Jake had let go and David sank to the carpet. There was one of Sybil with eight-year-old David; he was standing on the dock, wearing a bulky life vest, grasping his mother's hand. I shuffled through page after page of that innocent face grinning into my camera: the loose smile, the flat nose, low broad forehead, muddy brown eyes. I came across a photo of Grace helping David hold a fishing pole, her hand over his, winding the reel. And one taken just last summer of David at the Rockland Lobster Festival, wearing the T-shirt Grace and I had bought him.

When I saw that picture I wept again, my tears blotting the smile on David's face. Closing the covers of the album, I kicked it under the bed. Then I slid from the bed to the floor, pulling the bedspread around me, cuddling in it. Sitting huddled in pink chenille, my head leaning against the bed frame, I fingered the fringe of the bedspread. After several hours, I forced myself to stand, unwrapping the bedspread and letting it fall around my feet. I was stiff from sitting on the floor, my back hurt, and I was fed up with myself.

That afternoon Jake stopped by, but when he came onto the porch and knocked on the front door, I refused to answer. His rapping grew louder, pounding until the door rattled on its hinges, but I wouldn't let him in. The door stayed locked with the curtain drawn over the window panel. After I heard him clumping off the porch, I drew the curtain aside and watched his truck pull away. David was turned around in the passenger seat, his nose pressed against the back window, staring back at my cottage.

Quickly, I closed the curtain, trying to blot out the pitiful look I'd seen on David's face. He was so used to being with me whenever he wanted during the summer months, coming and going from my cottage as if it were his own home. He wouldn't understand why I didn't want to see him now. David would never make the connection between Grace's accident and my anger at him.

When I couldn't hear Jake's truck any more, I went into the bedroom and took Grace's blue fishing hat down from the mirror frame. I put it on my own head and stood looking at myself in the glass. Suddenly, it seemed the cottage walls were closing in on me, and I couldn't stand to be inside one minute longer.

Down at the cove, the sea was at mid-tide and the little beach was littered with seaweed. Still wearing Grace's hat, I knelt in the sand, facing the ocean.

The next evening after supper Sue showed up at my cottage, carrying a bottle of wine. I was in the garden, listlessly pulling weeds and staking the dahlias. I jumped when I heard her voice behind me.

"Don't you answer your phone these days?"

I swung around and saw her standing over me, the lowering sun behind her frizzy hair. "Oh, hi."

"That's it? 'Oh hi?' I've been trying to call you for three days and all you say is 'oh hi'? No explanation?"

"Maybe the phone's not working," I lied, pulling off my gardening gloves.

"Or maybe you weren't picking it up. Is everything okay?"

I didn't answer.

"Martha?"

"Everything's fine," I said, getting up and brushing the knees of my jeans.

"Good. Then you'll help me drink this. It's all the way from Napa Valley. Remember the conference I went to in San Francisco? Well, one of the pharmaceutical salesmen I met there sent me several bottles from the Mondavi Winery."

"That was nice," I said.

"No. Just good business." Sue studied me more closely. "You're not all right. Look at those dark circles under your eyes." She gently pressed her thumbs under my eyes.

I shook her off. "Do you want to open that bottle, or what?"

She didn't let my attitude stop her. "I was thinking of a sail. You can bring along a corkscrew. And a couple of paper cups."

I stood with my hands on my hips, looking out over the sea. I was about to tell Sue to go sailing without me, but then I got mad at myself. "Paper?" I said. "I'll bring the real thing. Let me grab 'em."

"Well, that's the spirit!"

It was nearly seven by the time we got *Remedy* underway. Outside the harbor, we sailed for an hour. At first Sue tried to engage me in conversation, but I didn't feel like talking. After a while, she gave up trying and concentrated on handling the tiller and the sails, navigating toward Rock Neck, where we planned to stop and have our wine.

I'd been so lost in my own thoughts, I hardly noticed the blanket of fog descending on us.

"I think we should head back." Sue's voice jolted me out of my private inner world. I detected a note of urgency in her words.

"What's wrong?" I asked.

"This fog's only going to get worse. We don't want to get caught in it."

"Do you think it's anything to worry about?"

"Not yet, but it could get that way in a hurry." Sue's face was grim as she brought the sloop about.

She was right. The fog was quickly becoming thicker. We hadn't gone far when we hit a solid bank of it. "Let the sail down, Martha! Before we ram into something."

I quickly dropped the mainsail, and Sue let down the anchor. The sea had changed from a slight ripple to flat calm, still as glass. The fog was denser and damp, fast becoming an impenetrable veil. From where we stood in the cockpit, we could no longer see the bow. I groped around and clutched the railing.

"Damn!" Sue said. "These nighttime fogs don't let up either. We could be sitting here until morning."

"Will that be safe?" I asked.

"We don't have much choice, Martha. It's too dangerous to get underway—we'd be sailing blind. We'd better go below and wait it out. It'll be drier there." Sue's voice sounded strangely flat, deadened by the fog. "You go on down. I'll check the anchor line—make sure it's secure."

"You convinced me," I said, opening the hatchway. I climbed down to the small cabin where two bunks met in a V toward the fore. The basket we'd brought with us sat on one of the bunks. I pulled out the bottle of wine and the two glasses that were tucked into the cloth-lined hamper. Then I sat down, leaned back, and peered out the porthole. Couldn't see a thing. Night and the fog had fallen simultaneously, like a lead curtain. And everything was strangely quiet, as if we were shut off from the world. A fog buoy moaned in the distance. I hoped we were out of the line of traffic, though it was not likely any vessels would be moving tonight.

When Sue came down the companionway, I sat up quickly and banged my head on the bulkhead. Her sweater was pearled with fog droplets. Even her hair was misted with the dampness, and even frizzier than usual. "Should I open this?" I asked, holding up the bottle of wine. "Might warm us up."

"Yes, please. God, I feel like such a fool for getting us stuck out here." Sue shrugged off the wet sweater. Smoothing out her turtleneck and tucking it into her white cotton slacks, she said, "I should have seen that damn fog coming."

"Hey, it happened all of a sudden. We just ran into it without any real warning. We'll be okay here, won't we?"

"Let's hope so. I left the running lights on."

I pulled the corkscrew from the basket and began to uncork the bottle of Merlot. Sue held out the glasses while I filled them.

She sipped hers, then took a deep sigh as she sank down on the other bunk.

"Hey, relax," I urged. "We're here, we can't go anywhere. We might as well enjoy it."

"I guess you've got a point there." Sue took a deeper taste of her wine, then leaned back. "Though you haven't exactly been a barrel of laughs today."

"Sorry. I had my mind on something, that's all."

"Well, we've got plenty of time. Want to talk about it?"

I tossed around in my head how much to tell her. I wanted to, but couldn't. "Maybe, sometime." I held out my empty glass to her. "This is smooth," I said. She refilled our glasses, and we drank in silence, listening to the sea slosh against the hull.

"This chill is right down to my bones," Sue said, hugging herself and shivering.

"Come over here and sit with me. That will help." Sue moved over to my bunk, sitting between my legs with her back to me. I pulled a blanket over us and wrapped my arms around her. "Better?" I asked.

"A little. Look if I doze off, just poke me or something."

"Go ahead and close your eyes. We'll take turns," I told her. "I'll take the first watch while you rest."

Sue leaned her head back against my chest. "Keep your ears open for any boat horns. I'll just nap for a minute." In no time, she was asleep in my arms. I held her until sunrise, when the fog lifted enough for us to make our way back to the harbor.

Days later, I was leaving the Hailey Harbor post office just as Jake was coming in. Each of us had a hand on the heavy door between us. He looked like hell: deep pouches under his eyes, gray stubble on his chin, the lines on his face etched even deeper than usual. I dropped my eyes from his and went out the door.

Instead of going into the post office, Jake followed me to the sidewalk. He put his hand on my elbow to stop me from getting into my car. "Martha, we've gotta clear up this mess between us."

I snapped, "Talking won't settle a damn thing."

"That don't sound like you. Ain't you the one who's always wanting to thrash things over, dump everything out in the open?"

"Okay, I'll tell you what's been on my mind." I turned around and looked my brother in the eye. "I'm worried that David might be a danger to someone else."

Jake swiped at the air. "Nonsense," he said. "Chrissakes, David wouldn't hurt a mosquito."

"But look what happened to Grace!"

Jake kicked angrily at a piece of concrete that had broken off the sidewalk. "That was just an accident. Could happen to anyone."

Furious at the way he kept denying David's part in what had happened to Grace, I clutched the collar of his shirt. "Look at this realistically, Jake! David grabbed Grace and that's what made her fall."

He brushed my hand away. "He just got upset, is all. David didn't mean for Grace to fall."

"Maybe not, but he did grab her necklace. And that's what made her lose her balance. What if David loses his temper like that again sometime and hurts someone else?"

Without saying anything more, Jake shook his head and

started walking away, headed back toward the post office.

"We're talking about something serious here, Jake! Maybe even manslaughter."

He came back and leaned into my face. "Don't ever say that!" Sid Hutch was walking our way along the sidewalk. Jake nodded his head at him, waited until he was well past us, then added in a lowered voice, "Never. You hear? Sonofabitching never."

"This is something serious we're dealing with here," I said. "You can't protect David forever. Maybe we ought to tell Sue. Or Chancey. As sheriff, he should know what really happened last fall."

"Goddamnit! Don't you breathe a word of it! Nobody needs to know but you, me, and David." Jake took hold of my shoulders. "Look at me, Martha. You've gotta promise not to tell what happened out there. Not ever. You tell Chancey, and before you know it the state's gonna step in and try to tell me what's best for my own boy. Those candy-ass boys from over to the mainland, in their pretty suits and neckties, will come over here and haul him away. I won't have no say in it."

"Jake, listen. David needs to be watched closely. All the time."

"Goddamnit, Martha, you sound like he ought to be locked up in Thomaston. Kept in jail the rest of his life."

"That's not what I'm saying at all," I insisted.

"What then? You want him in some frigging institution? Like that damn hell hole we visited once?"

"Jake, look, I just want us all to be safe. David too."

"Bullshit. What do you know about it anyway? What's best for him? Chrissakes, you come prancing in here for a few months a year and try to tell us how to run our lives. Just go back to your fancy city and quit sticking your nose in our business. Leave David to me." At that, Jake walked away from me, for good this time.

I slumped against my car. "What about Grace?" I called after him, my eyes burning with tears. "If you know so much, why did you let Grace die?"

A knock on the screen door startled me. I shoved aside the postcard I'd been writing to Yolanda, a friend in Boston, and went out to the sun porch. The sheriff was outside, wearing his brown uniform, standing with one foot on the porch step. "Something wrong, Chancey?" I asked through the screen.

"See now, don't get upset, but David's been in an accident."

I felt my face drain.

"Now, take it easy," he said, opening the door and coming onto the porch. "He's gonna be all right."

"For God's sake, what happened?"

"Nearly drowned, down at the bridge."

I gasped. "David fell in?"

"Nobody can figure out how it happened, see. You know how Jake's always at him to be careful." Chancey hooked his thumbs into his belt. "Anyways, there was a splash and next thing anybody knew, David's thrashing around in the raceway. Tide was rushing in like crazy and David couldn't keep afloat, from what Harry Parsons told me. He was wearing rubber bibs and they must of filled up with water—that'll add a hundred pounds to your weight, see, and pull you down."

"But he's going to be okay?"

"That other boy—the one who tried to kill himself early in the summer?—he jumped in and saved him."

"Ben?"

"Damn smart of him, too. Tied a rope around the railing, see, then around his own waist and jumped in. Got David under the arms, he did, and brought him up to the surface."

"Where was Jake when all this was happening?"

"Over to the Seagull's Nest having a cup of coffee. He saw all the commotion and come running out to the bridge like a bat outta hell. Jake and some of the other men grabbed the rope and pulled both boys in." Chancey lifted his hat and wiped the sweat from his brow, then he set the hat back on his head. "Damn lucky, when you think of it. Your nephew would be a goner now 'cept that other boy was a quick thinker."

"Where's David now?"

"Up to the clinic. Doctor Sue is trying to get him warmed up a bit. Says hypothermia can set in awfully fast, and she wants to make sure his body temperature is normal, see. Of course, as the shock started wearing off, David got more and more agitated. It took both Doc Sue and Jake to get him calmed down. When I left, she was getting ready to give him a tranquilizer. I expect Jake'll take him back home when they get him in shape." Chancey hitched his belt over his enormous stomach. "See now, I can't remember ever seeing Jake so shook up. He sure does think a lot of that boy of his, doesn't he?"

I nodded, feeling numb. "And Ben? Where's he?"

"I dropped him back at the Tuttle house, see. He was pretty quiet about his part in the rescue. Kinda shy like, isn't he?"

As soon as Chancey left, I drove over to Jake's. I stood in the yard, taking in the old family house. Everything Jake and I had shared here as children swam before my eyes: the

Christmas we both got double-blade skates and our father made an ice pond for us in the yard. The summer we built a go-cart; I hammered the body together and Jake put on the wheels and axle, then we added side mirrors that we'd stolen off an abandoned car at the town dump. For Jake's first date, with Mary Ellen Adamson when he was a junior in high school, I taught him how to jitterbug. Weeks before the school dance, we practiced together in the living room, pushing the sofa and chairs back against the wall and playing 45's on a record player.

I thought of how, after our father drowned, Jake took care of our mother; even after he married Sybil, Mother lived with them until she got pancreatic cancer and died. I remembered a summer when the bluefish were running—Jake and Grace went fishing, and then we all had a feast over a fondue pot, rolling chunks of the delicious white meat in beer batter and dunking them in hot oil.

Now, standing in the yard with my back to the cove, I looked up at the cupola on top of the house. As kids, Jake and I had often waited up there, watching through the windows for our father to come in from the sea, worried that he might not come home.

I went inside the house; in the foyer, I heard the familiar tick of the grandfather clock. Climbing the stairs, I opened the door to David's room. He was huddled in his bed, lying on his stomach. Jake knelt on the floor on one knee, awkwardly rubbing his son's back. David was hiccuping and moaning into his pillow, "Water cold, Papa. I drown."

I knelt on the floor beside my brother. Reaching out my hand, I placed it over his, helping him rub David's back.

Jake was crying. There'd been only two other times I'd seen him cry. Once was when Sybil died. The other was when David fell down the stairs, around the age of seven or eight. Jake had been scolding David about leaving the water running in the upstairs bathroom sink; as Jake nagged at him, wagging his finger, David kept backing up. At the top of the stairs, he tripped and tumbled head over heels. Grace and I had been in the living room talking with Sybil; at the clattering sound, we rushed into the foyer. Jake was leaping down the stairs. At the landing, he leaned over his son and saw that he'd put his teeth through his lower lip and was bleeding. That was when Jake started to sob, ducking his head, trying to hide his tears from us. Scooping David in his arms, he carried him outside to the truck and drove to the island clinic.

Now, Jake swiped hard at his eyes with the back of his hand. Pulling a handkerchief from his back pocket, he loudly blew his nose. He sat on the edge of David's bed and patted his leg. I sat in the maple rocker beside the bed, and asked softly, "How's my boy?"

"Not good," David sniffled into the pillow. His hiccuping was letting up, and he was beginning to quiet down. "Papa?" he whimpered.

"Papa's right here," Jake said. "Auntie Martha's here too. Don't you worry none."

After a while, David fell asleep, and Jake motioned for me to follow him out of the room. In the hallway, instead of taking the main staircase down to the foyer, he turned and headed toward the back set of stairs that led up to the cupola. I trailed him up the narrow flight of steps into the tiny windowed room. Two dusty wooden rockers faced the cove, and we each sat in one. Then—the way we had as children—we linked our fingers together, swinging our hands between us as we rocked, and watched the sun set over the cove.

I slept overnight in my old room and had just gone down to the kitchen when I heard David coming down too, taking the steps one at a time the way a child does.

The night before, Jake had listened to the radio for news of the weather and discovered that the early part of the day was predicted to be calm but that the wind would pick up later. He felt torn, trying to decide if he should stay home with David in the morning or haul traps before the sea got rough. August was a prime season for lobster, and I knew he couldn't afford to stay in from fishing. So when Ben called around nine last evening to ask if he should be at the dock in the morning as usual, I urged Jake to say yes.

I went out in the hall to meet David. He was standing on the next-to-last step, gripping the banister with both hands. "David, what's the matter?" I asked, laying my hands over his. His grip was tight.

"Fall in deep water. Cold. I scared."

Climbing the stair, I wrapped my arms around him and leaned into his back. "You're warm now, sweetheart. You're safe here."

"I safe?"

"Yes. Auntie Martha is going to spend the morning with you." Reaching around him, I pried his fingers loose from the rail, then led him down the step and into the kitchen. "How about some cocoa? That'll take the last of the chill out." I poured a cup of hot chocolate from the saucepan on the stove and carried the cup to the table. "Come, sit down now and drink this while it's hot." I pulled out a chair for him, and he sat down heavily. Holding the cup to his lips I said, "Here. Blow on it first."

He pursed his lips and blew over the steaming cup.

"That's good. Now drink up." I set the cup in his hands, but he still didn't take a sip.

"Need 'mallow, Marfa."

"Oh sure, how could I forget?" In the pantry I found a bag of marshmallows, probably left over from a Fourth of July bonfire. I dropped two of them into David's cup and they began to melt into foam.

He slurped the hot chocolate. Then, with froth covering his top lip like a mustache, he asked, "Where Papa at?"

"Papa's working. Like he does every morning."

"Ben work too? My Bennybuddy?"

"Yes." I set a platter onto the table and sat down beside him. "Here, have a woodchuck sandwich," I said, fitting thick slices of bacon into a folded piece of buttered toast.

David took a big bite. With his mouth full, he asked, "I go work?"

"You can help Papa unload the boat when he comes in."

After breakfast, I drew a tub of hot water. David soaked in the tub, playing with a plastic boat and a squirt gun. Then he shaved with his electric razor. When he came out of the bathroom, his hair was still wet and he was barefoot. He was wearing a white T-shirt and green work pants without a belt. "Fix your shirt," I said. "You've got it on wrong side out."

He took it off, mussing up his hair in the process, and put it back on properly. I combed his hair down with my fingers and tied his black canvas sneakers after he put them on.

We went upstairs together, and I helped David clean his room. Then I sat on his bed and darned some of his socks while he listened to tapes on his boombox: John Denver, Garth Brooks, Kenny Rogers. David flipped cassettes in and out of his boombox, listening to a song halfway through, slapping his knee to the music, then changing to another song.

I had no way of knowing if everything would ever be completely all right between Jake and me again, but I still felt comfortable being in this house. So many memories here. Whatever happened, I'd always have those good memories of Jake and me growing up here as island kids.

It might be fun now, I thought, to look through the trunk in the attic where I stored yearbooks and other mementos.

David and I went up to the attic. Against one slanting wall was a chest I'd built when I was a teenager. I'd stained and varnished it, and finished it with brass fittings. Over the years, I'd stowed all kinds of things in there. I opened the chest, leaning the hinged top against the sloping rafters.

David had never before been allowed to look inside the chest and he was excited, shifting from foot to foot, clapping his hands. "Big stuff," he said.

"It is a lot of stuff, isn't it?" I said as I rummaged through the contents, yanking out a letter sweater I'd earned in high school basketball and tossing it onto the floor. I uncovered a bronze medallion tied to a red-white-and-blue ribbon. It was one I'd won at a consolidated island track competition. As soon as David spotted it, he snatched it. "Wait a minute, that's not yours," I said. But he clutched it and held it tightly against his chest. I thought, what the heck, why not let him hold it? What harm could it do?

Sitting down on the floor, cross-legged, David rubbed the ribbon between his fingers and fiddled with the bronze medal. He flipped the medallion from palm to palm, pressed it between thumb and finger, kissed it, and even put it up to his ear.

I watched him try to fit it over his neck. The ribbon got hung up on the brim of his soft red hat, and he became frustrated. "I no can do," he screeched, biting down hard on the edge of the medallion.

Damn, I never should have let him take it in the first place. What had I started? "Give that to me, David."

Quickly, he swung his arms behind his back hiding the medallion. "I want."

Taking a deep breath, I squatted on the floor in front of him. "Look, David. You're going to have to learn. You can't take things that don't belong to you. Give it to me."

"Annh annh annh. Mine. Mine." He shook his head so vigorously, the hat fell off his head.

For just a moment, I felt afraid. David was a good-sized man. And strong. I didn't know what his temper might make him do. I wished Jake were here; I didn't know if I would be able to get the medal from David by myself. But it seemed that I should try. Steeling myself, I said with as much authority as I could, "David! I'm not fooling. When I say give it to me, I mean this minute." Kneeling in front of him, I stretched my arms around him, reaching behind his back. I was able to feel the medal in his fist. "Give it here, David," I said as I tried to pry it free.

"No!" He gripped it even more tightly.

I worked my fingers into his fist, trying to pry the medal loose. We struggled for several minutes. If anyone had seen us, they might have thought we were hugging. Just as I was about to give up and try something else, I felt his grip loosen. Quickly, I grabbed the medal from him and pulled it free.

When I leaned back on my heels, David raised his arm as if to strike me.

At first I flinched. Then I jumped to my feet and grabbed his wrist. "Don't you dare! Don't you ever, ever hit me. Do you understand? Never hit anyone!" I said, staring down at him.

He struggled to pull his arm away from me. When he couldn't get free, he started to bite my hand to make me let go.

"Oh no, you don't!" I squeezed his wrist more tightly

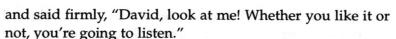

and said firmly, "David, look at me! Whether you like it or not, you're going to listen."

His eyes darted wildly, and a string of drool dripped from the corner of his mouth.

"David," I insisted, "look at Aunt Martha!" I bent my face close to his so that he had no choice but to look at me. Softening my voice, I said, "That's better. Now, I'm going to put this back where we got it. And you're going to leave it there." I buried the medal in the trunk.

David folded his arms and scowled, but I didn't think he'd cause any more trouble.

"Good boy." I set his hat on his head, pulled the string on the overhead light bulb, and led him, still sulking, downstairs.

In the afternoon we walked down to the dock at Old Cove to meet *The Sybil*. As we got close to the water, David became terrified, and he refused to walk down the catwalk to the floating wharf. "I drown, I drown," he kept whimpering.

Just inside the fish house was hanging a faded orange life jacket, splotched with oil stains. I took it outside and buckled it onto him. "Come on, I'll hold your hand. You won't fall in," I promised, starting to walk down the ramp. David followed hesitantly, with me tugging his hand. "That's right. You're doing great," I kept reassuring him. It seemed forever before we made it to the bottom and stepped onto the dock. Immediately, David sat down, planting himself squarely in the middle. I watched *The Sybil* enter the cove, slow her wake, and make her way toward us. Ben was at the wheel.

When *The Sybil* pulled up, David still wouldn't budge. He sat huddled on the dock, his arms wrapped around the bulky lifejacket. Jake tossed me the bowline, which I wrapped around a cleat. Jumping off the boat onto the dock, he tied the stern line, then knelt on one knee to talk with David.

Ben stepped out of the wheelhouse, but ducked back inside as soon as he spotted me. We hadn't seen each other or talked since he'd left my house in such a rage weeks ago. Now I needed to tell him how grateful I was that he'd rescued David, so I went aboard. He was pretending to be busy, using a rag to wipe down the instruments—CB radio, depth finder, fuel gauges.

"I don't know how to thank you, Ben."

Clearing the cluttered console, he crumpled one of Jake's empty cigarette packages and tossed it into a pail of trash before he asked, "What for?"

"For pulling David out of the water."

"Oh, that. No big deal," he said, blushing. "Anybody would've done the same thing."

"But it *was* a big deal," I insisted. "Very big. You saved his life."

He met my eyes briefly, then shrugged his shoulders and turned to hang his oilskin bibs on a hook. I thought the conversation was over, but as I was stepping off *The Sybil*, he blurted, "Now we're even."

CHAPTER 12

I spent the rest of the afternoon down at the cove in front of my cottage, working on my small fishing boat. It took some struggling, but I managed to set the boat, hull facing up, on sawhorses next to the boathouse. A spot of dry rot had started in the peak of the bow, and I wanted to get rid of it before it spread. Digging away the rotted wood, I replaced it with fiberglass filler.

While I was working, I kept thinking of Ben. He'd looked so thin. His face seemed lined with sadness. For the past few weeks, I'd kept my distance from him, thinking that was what he wanted. And, feeling too like I needed a break from his troubles. But now, after seeing how sad he looked, I grew more and more worried.

It was getting dark by the time I walked to the Tuttle house, carrying a blueberry cake. Only a light in the kitchen was shining. Through the windowpane in the back door, I could see Ben sitting at the table. He seemed surprised to see me when he opened the door to my knock.

Holding the cake pan out to him, I said, "I picked blue-

berries a few days ago. I thought it'd be nice to have someone to share this with."

Still blocking the doorway, Ben said, "I'm not really
hungry."

"For my cake? You've got to be kidding." I pushed past
him into the kitchen. "Let's see, we'll need a knife, a couple
of plates, forks. I don't suppose you have any coffee?"

He pulled the door shut and came toward me, taking
the cake pan I held out to him. "Coffee's been sitting in the
pot all day," he grumbled.

"That'll be fine." I got plates from the cupboard while
Ben re-heated the coffee and poured a mug for me. "Here," I
said handing him his plate. "This was my mother's recipe."

Pulling out a chair, Ben sat down and laid his hands on
the table. The calluses on his hands told me he'd been
working hard.

"Go ahead, give it a try," I said sitting down across from
him.

Ben smiled wanly and picked up the cake with his
hand, nodding his head as he chewed.

"The trick is to coat the blueberries with flour before
you mix them into the batter. Keeps them from sinking.
Then sprinkle sugar on the top before it goes into the oven.
Makes it crusty." Ben licked his fingers and cut himself
another slice.

I sipped at the black, stale coffee. "Ben," I said, "I need
to make something clear between us. I wasn't reading your
journal again."

He searched my face, took a drink of water from his
mug, then set his cup down on the table. "Whatever."

"It's the truth." I took another sip of coffee, but it tasted
awful. "There is something I have to ask you, though." Reaching
into my pants pocket, I held out his ring. "Is this yours?"

Ben's face blanched. "I figured you had that! I saw the picture in your darkroom." He grabbed the gold band from me. "Where'd you find it?"

"On the beach. The day after your accident."

"You can say it straight out. We both know it was no accident."

"Okay then. The day after you cut your wrist," I said. "I meant to tell you about it sooner. What's it mean anyway, that ring?"

"I was gonna throw that fucking thing in the ocean." Ben flicked the ring angrily with his fingernail and watched it skitter across the floor.

"What's your father want from you?" I asked.

"Everything. At graduation he told me, 'Now you can be a true witness for Christ.' He's always quoting the Bible, you know, so he says, 'The fear of the Lord is the beginning of knowledge and wisdom.' That's from Proverbs. Then he goes, 'You remember that and you're ready to stand beside me and serve the Lord.'"

"I'm still not sure I understand how the ring fits into all this."

"See the cross here on the front? My father told me 'Serve me and you serve God.' So the ring's just a way to make me remember who's the boss."

"God?"

"My old man!"

"He's built himself a little dynasty with that church." I poured my coffee into the sink. I set the kettle on the stove then leaned against the counter. Standing behind him, I was struck again at how thin Ben had become. He sat hunched in the chair. "Tea bags?" I asked. "I can get one. Just tell me where."

He pointed to the cupboard over the stove. "First shelf."

I carried my cup back to the table. "The end of the summer's nearly here."

"Yeah, and then what?" He stared at the ring on the floor.

"Ben, what do *you* want?"

"I don't know." He spread his hands and gazed at his fingernails, chipped and lined with dirt. "I like what I've been doing with Jake. Working on the boat and all."

"Why don't you stay, then? I don't know how much Jake can afford to pay you, but I know he enjoys having you on board. In fact, I think he's come to depend on you. He won't admit he's starting to get arthritic. Aches and pains. I can see it in the way he walks. And there's a limit to how much David can do."

"I don't see any way I can stay on the island. The Tuttles are selling this house. You knew that, didn't you? I guess someone from Philadelphia is buying it."

"I knew it was for sale, but I didn't know it'd sold. How much more painting do you have to do?"

"It'll be finished by next week. Just need to do the rest of the trim and the shutters. Then my job will be done and I'll have to leave."

"That's a shame. For you to leave, I mean."

"What else can I do? I can't really afford to rent anywhere."

"I don't know how you feel about it, but you *could* stay at my place again," I said. "It'd be okay with me."

Ben glanced down at the tabletop, rubbing his fingers on the smooth Formica.

"I promise never to snoop in your things, you know, Ben."

He didn't say anything, just tossed me a skeptical look.

"You can stay there if you want," I went on. "I'll be leaving around Labor Day, going back to Boston. But the cottage doesn't really need to be closed up for winter until, oh, say, October? Maybe by then you'll have something else figured out."

He tapped his chin with his knuckle, thinking. "I don't know if that's best."

"Oh, well, maybe you'd rather go on living under your father's thumb. You want him to keep his hooks in you?"

He looked toward the floor again at the ring, then picked it up. "No," he said, juggling the ring in his hand. He folded his fist over it, his knuckles whitening. His voice was firmer and more decisive than I'd ever heard it. "I want that bastard out of my life."

"Good. Tell *him* that."

Early Sunday morning, as we had planned, I bought two tickets for the ferry. As I walked out of the terminal, I looked for Ben's old Bonneville in the long line of cars and trucks waiting to board. He was parked near the edge of the lot where the line snaked back onto the road. The car looked as if Ben had been doing some bodywork on it and had patches of gray primer paint along the rocker panels and fenders. I rapped on the driver's side window. When he rolled it down, I asked, "You sure it's okay to take your car over to the mainland?"

"No problem." As I walked around and opened the door on the passenger side, Ben tossed some empty Pepsi cans and Hershey Bar wrappers into the back seat. After I climbed in, he turned the key several times—the ignition coughed, halted, coughed again, finally caught—and he drove onto the ferry.

Ben didn't talk much on the crossing; he seemed deep in thought, gazing out at the sea as we sat on the top deck. When the ferry docked in Rockland, we got back into his car and drove off the boat. From Belfast we headed inland and slightly northwest. As we got closer and closer to

Bangor, Ben grew even more quiet, and he kept biting his lip and drumming his fingers on the steering wheel.

"Want to stop for breakfast? We have time." I pointed to the clock on the dashboard. "It's only quarter past ten. Didn't you tell me church gets out around eleven?"

"Yeah. I guess we have time if that's what you want to do. There's a place just around the corner from the church." Ben drove down Union Street, pulled into the parking lot of a tired looking doughnut shop.

I said, "How about that booth over there in the corner?" Ben didn't answer, just headed for the booth. "What would you like?" I asked as we sat down across from each other.

"Juice, I guess. Orange juice. Maybe a raised dough- nut." He started to pull out his wallet.

"I'll get it." I put in the order for Ben and got a glass of milk and a muffin for myself. I set my glass down and asked, "Why don't you like milk? Are you allergic to dairy products or something?"

Ben played with his juice glass, twirling it between the palms of his hands. "It's a long story," he sighed. "Like everything else, it has to do with my father."

How thick could I be? Of course! He meant the incident he wrote about in his diary—his father selfishly drinking his mother's milk after the baby died. I balled up my nap- kin and tossed it onto the table. "Maybe it's time to do what we came here to do."

"Got to sometime," Ben said. "Might as well do it now and get it over with."

Leaving Ben's car in the doughnut shop parking lot, we walked the short distance to the Lamp of Faith Church Ministries. Overhead, a jet marred the blue sky with a wispy white line. "That's it," Ben said, pointing, as we rounded the corner. "My father's castle."

We waited on the sidewalk across from the squat white building that looked like it might have once been a store of some sort. People drifted out from the building, pausing to shake hands with Pastor Ralph. I was surprised at how ordinary he looked. He was a tall man, and his demeanor seemed pleasant. Standing on the top step, wearing a brown suit and a peach-colored tie, he grabbed hands and pumped them in a friendly way, smiling all the time.

Ben's mother, Sister Harriet, stood slightly behind him. She was a gaunt woman, with long graying hair held back on each side with combs. She wore a gray cotton dress down to her ankles, and a hand-knit gray shawl that hung in feathery fringes. Like a little gray bird, I thought.

I heard Ben catch his breath, and I glanced over at him. His jaw was clenched, and a blush was spreading up from his neck. When I moved closer and slipped my arm around his back, he relaxed a little.

Ben had put the ring in an envelope, which he was carrying in the pocket of his green windbreaker. Recognizing a young boy from a Bible study class he'd led, Ben called him over. "Jamie, take this to my father, will you?" He handed the envelope to the boy and ruffled his hair. "Okay?"

"Hi, Brother Ben. Why weren't you in church this morning?" The boy took the envelope and held it by the corner, so that the ring shifted. "You want me to give this to Pastor Ralph?"

"Yeah. After everybody leaves. Before he goes back inside the church." Reaching into his jeans pocket, Ben pulled out a crumpled dollar bill. "Here, buy yourself a candy bar or something."

"Thanks, Ben!" Jamie looked up and down the street at the cars pulling out from the parking lot. Then he darted across, stood on the sidewalk, and watched the rest of the fellowship straggle out.

As the last one, an elderly man with a cane, made his way down the steps, Jamie looked back at us and Ben nodded to him. "Now," he mouthed.

Jamie dashed up the steps and handed the envelope to Ben's father, who opened it and looked at the contents. They exchanged a few words, and then the boy pointed to Ben. Both Pastor Ralph and Sister Harriet looked across the street, and Harriet's hand flew to her mouth. She started toward Ben, but her husband held her back, his hand on her arm.

Then Pastor Ralph came down the steps and strode across the street. Watching him, Ben began jiggling his leg and rubbing the mole over his eyebrow. I stood right next to him for support.

As he approached, Pastor Ralph held up the envelope, a smile on his face. "What's it mean, Ben, giving me this?"

"Looks like you had a good turnout for church today, sir," Ben stammered, his eyes looking everywhere but at his father. "And that little Jamie has grown just these few months I've been away, hasn't he? Two inches, I bet."

Pastor Ralph rested his hand on Ben's shoulder. Though Ben was tall, his father towered over him. "Too bad you missed the service. We had some good singing. Well, now that you're back you can come lead the Bible study on Wednesday. And help out with the service next Sunday."

"Sir. I c-c-can't do that, sir."

Pastor Ralph's smile disappeared. "Why not?"

"I'm not staying. Not coming home."

"What do you mean, not coming home? Not coming back to the parsonage? Or not coming back to Bangor at all? You can't stay out there on that island forever." Then he said, in a voice that was an attempt at humor, "Painting a house! What kind of work is that anyway?"

Traffic rolled past on the street. Ben's mother stood on

the church stairs, gripping the handrail as if to hold herself back from flying over to her son. Poor little gray sparrow, I thought, watching her.

Pastor Ralph leaned in closer to Ben and said in a conspiratorial tone, "You come back here, son, and work in *God's house*, where you belong."

Ben's head was lowered and his voice was barely loud enough to be heard. "I'm not going to work for your church."

"Don't turn away from Jesus, son. Your soul's at stake here." Pastor Ralph's eyes seemed to fill, but he turned away quickly and I couldn't be sure. For a brief moment I felt sorry for him, and this thought crossed my mind: maybe he's just as unsure as the rest of us. Maybe all the unbending religion and hard rules and strict discipline is just his way of trying to make sense of life, of trying to create some order in this chaotic world.

But I didn't feel sorry for him for long. When he turned back to us, any sign of softness had vanished from his face. His eyes were hard, his mouth a thin line. "Son," he said, one arm in a tight grip around Ben's shoulders, "think of your salvation. If you leave the church, you know what will happen. Demons will harass you. You'll lose power with God."

Ben swallowed hard.

Just then I spoke up. "Ben, don't feel pressured."

Pastor Ralph threw me an impatient glance. "Who are you?"

"An island neighbor . . ."

Brushing away my words, he said, "This is between my son and me. Between Ben and God."

I stepped closer to his father. "I just want Ben to do what he thinks is best."

None of us had heard Ben's mother cross the street. We didn't realize she was behind us until she timidly placed her hand on her son's back. "Hello, Benny."

"Hi, Mom," Ben said tenderly, looking down at her.

"I've missed you, Bennie," she said, pulling her shawl tight across her scrawny breasts. "I'm glad you've come home."

"Well, I don't know yet . . ." Ben rubbed the mole over his eyebrow.

"It's lonely at home with you gone," she said. "Awful quiet."

"I have to think about it, Mom." Ben seemed to be weakening.

"Now Harriet, I told you to stay put. Run back along. You wait inside the church for me. I'll take care of this," said Pastor Ralph.

"But . . ." she protested in a timorous voice.

"No buts about it. I'll take care of the business at hand. You wait for me like I told you," he said in a stern voice.

She flew at Ben with a swift hug, then quickly withdrew. Wrapping her arms around herself, she cast him a plaintive look.

Ben reached toward his mother, his arms out. "Mom," he said again, his voice choking. But then he dropped his arms and buried his hands in his pockets.

She gave him one more long look, taking him in, before she started across the street. Several times she halted and glanced back at her son.

"See what you've done to your mother. Got her all worked up. Now, you take this ring and come along with us." Pastor Ralph held the envelope out to his son.

Ben's eyes darted from his father, to me, and back again. He seemed to hesitate, but finally he stammered, "I c-c-can't. I'm going to stay on Quarry Island."

With a slow and deliberate motion, the pastor lifted his arm from Ben's shoulder. He stepped back and, while surveying his son, smoothed his tie and straightened his suit coat. His eyes narrowed as he said, "I'll give you six months to change your mind. If you're not back home by then, back in the fold where you belong, I won't have any choice. I'll have to put you out of the fellowship." He held the envelope in the air. "You take this now and pray on it. Ask God to deliver you." He pitched the envelope, but Ben didn't reach for it and it landed on the curb. The ring fell out and rolled into the street as a St. Johnsbury semi, heading north on Union Street, drove by. We watched the gold band as it spun under the truck and just missed being crushed by the heavy double tires.

Ben's father pointed to the ring as it rolled into the ditch. "See there? That's what happens when you disobey God." He marched across the street, grabbed Sister Harriet by the waist, and disappeared inside the tiny store-front church.

CHAPTER 13

Everyone on the island was tracking the hurricane. The storm had moved west across the Atlantic Ocean, then turned north. Though it looked at first as though it might miss land altogether, it veered inland and brushed Nantucket, killing two people. Now it was stalled over Cape Cod, and we worried that the storm would continue into Maine. We hoped that if the hurricane did reach us it would be mostly spent, just a residue of strong winds and rain. If we were lucky, it would move out to sea and miss us all together.

For two days the sky had been dark and threatening, the wind picking up steadily, trees bending horizontally. The sea rolled with twelve-foot swells, and the surf crashed white and foamy against the granite shore. The fishermen had begun hauling smaller boats out of the water and securing larger boats on their moorings.

As the threat of the storm grew, I battened down my cottage. Ben showed up to help me fasten shutters and store away the Adirondack chairs and hammock. He said he'd taken down the scaffolding at the Tuttle house and had buttoned up the house. After he helped cover the daybed and wicker chair on my porch with tarps, he drove off toward Old Cove to give Jake a hand in securing *The Sybil*.

By evening, the rain hammered against the closed shutters of my cottage. The wind was screaming, and every so often a small twig broke off a nearby maple tree and clattered onto the roof. Pinecones twisted off trees and hurtled against the screens. I put fresh D batteries in my portable radio and flashlight, and set out extra batteries too.

As the sky got even darker, leaden with clouds, Jake phoned and suggested I come over and wait out the storm with him. I turned off all the lights in my cottage, grabbed the flashlight and radio, then drove the short distance to Old Cove. Hunched over the steering wheel, I strained to see out the windshield. The rain was coming down so hard that my wipers, even on high speed, couldn't keep up with the onslaught. In one place the road was flooded, and I didn't know if my Escort would make it through. The engine sputtered a little as I plowed my way through the deep puddle, water splashing to the bottom of my door. What a relief when I came around the corner and saw the lights from Jake's house! I parked haphazardly in the yard and dashed through the pounding rain into the house. As I hung my dripping slicker on a hook and pulled off my rubber boots, a murmur of voices and the smell of Jake's cigarette drifted out from the living room.

I walked into the room to find Ben sitting on the floor teaching David how to play *Go Fish*. Jake sat in an overstuffed chair with his feet propped on a coffee table littered with nautical charts and old newspapers. I patted his shoulder and he raised his hand in a wave. For the first time since earlier in the summer, the four of us were together.

"I'd say we got ourselves a big blow," Jake said as he ground out his cigarette. He picked up the remote for the TV, skipping through the channels until he found a Bangor station with a balding weatherman pointing out the storm's movement. The station flashed footage of the turmoil the hurricane had already left behind in Cape Cod: washed-out houses, torn-up docks, and smashed boats. I sat forward on the couch to get a better view and to hear the forecast over the voices of Ben and David as they finished their card game.

Wheel of Fortune came on, and David quit the card game. He sat on the floor, huddled close to the set, calling out letters. Ben wrapped a rubber band around the deck of cards, then joined me on the couch.

The rain stabbed sideways at the windows as the wind moaned and screamed. Suddenly the lights flickered and went out. As the television went black, David became frightened. "TV broke!" he screamed.

"We'll be all right, David," I reassured him. "Papa will find a lantern. Right, Jake?"

"Got some candles too. Ben, see if you can find them in the kitchen. Second drawer past the fridge. The matches are on the shelf over the stove. I'll get the kerosene lantern from the back hall."

Ben and Jake left the room to find some light. At my feet, David pulled at a strand of his hair and breathed heavily. "Hey, look at this," I told him. Holding the flashlight under my chin, I snapped it on. With the beam high-lighting my face, I stretched my mouth into an exaggerated smile. David smiled back weakly, and I handed the flashlight to him. "Here, you hold it."

David grabbed it with both hands. "I see." He pointed it around the room, the beam shining on objects then leaving them in shadows again.

While David was engrossed with the flashlight, I fumbled with the portable radio, turning the dial for a weather station. Jake came back into the room, set a kerosene lantern over the fireplace, and lit the wick.

"I found three candles," Ben said, coming into the room from the kitchen. When we'd placed the candles around the room, Jake said, "David, turn off that flashlight. Gotta save the batteries. Give it here, now."

"No, Papa. I blind!" David held the flashlight straight out in front of him, jabbing its laser beam around the room.

"Let him keep it, Jake," I said as I fiddled with the radio dial. Static came on, and we heard a female voice reporting: "Winds increasing, could whip up to gale force."

"Looks like the storm could go one way or the other," Jake said. "If it picks up to sixty-four knots, we got a real live hurricane on our hands."

"What did you do with *The Sybil*?" I asked.

"Doubled her up on the mooring, put bumpers on all sides. But she still could get chewed into toothpicks."

"I afraid dark," David whimpered.

"You aren't afraid with that flashlight on, are you?" I reassured him. "You've got lots of light there."

David shone the flashlight directly into my eyes. "Scoot over here with me," I said, sitting down on the floor and leaning against the couch.

David lay on his back with his head in my lap, holding the flashlight pointed up toward the ceiling. As I stroked his temples, he began to relax, even though the wind was howling outside. He grew more and more sleepy and had trouble keeping his eyes open. His eyes fell shut, then he forced them open, fell shut, forced them open. The flashlight began to tilt, its beam wavering on the ceiling and walls. Soon, the flashlight clunked onto the floor and I turned it off.

Jake dropped into the armchair and settled his feet on the coffee table. He lit a cigarette and said to Ben, "Sit down and take a load off. Might as well get comfortable. There's nothing to do now but wait it out."

As Ben took his place on the couch, I said, "Did you hear that Owen and Emily sold their house? Ben's going to have to move."

"That so?" Jake asked, looking at Ben.

"I'll probably go back to the mainland," Ben said. "Find a job there."

Jake eyed him steadily. "That what you want?"

"Not really. But I don't know what else to do."

Jake smoked the last few drags of his cigarette, then tamped it out in the ashtray. After a period of silence, he said, "There's one other thing to consider. I could keep you on as sternman. My old bones have got stiff and sore as hell. These last few years, I've had to back off on the number of traps I set out. With you on board, I could haul more." Jake coughed and cleared his throat, then said, "Fact is, I could use you to help out."

Ben took off his Red Sox cap, swatted it against his knee a couple of times, then twisted it in his hands. Looking at the cap as he spoke, he said, "Are you sure?"

"Jesus, you want the job or not?"

"Yeah." Ben hesitated, still nervously twisting his cap. "But, well, I . . ."

Shaking another Marlboro out of the pack, Jake said, "Spit it out, boy."

"You think I can do the work okay? I've screwed up a lot."

Jake tamped the cigarette on the arm of his chair. Instead of lighting it, he tapped it back into the pack, and dropped the pack into his shirt. "Let's clear up one thing," he said. "That day on the beach, with the knife and all? What was eating at you to make you want to do something like that?"

I reached up and squeezed Ben's knee to give him reassurance. Finally, he said, "My father . . . . I don't know. I can't explain it. It just felt like I wasn't ever going to get out from under him."

"Looks to me like you done it."

"What do you mean?"

"You been living here on the island all summer. I ain't seen your old man poking around anywhere, unless he's hiding out in the Tuttle's garage where you keep that old heap you call a car."

Rubbing his hands on the knees of his jeans, Ben shrugged.

"Could be it's between your ears where you can't get rid of him." Jake tapped his own forehead with his fingertip. "Right here. If that's where you're lugging your father around, then I'd say it's up to you to get him unstuck. Hardly pays for you to keep worrying about him, seeing how he is and all. I wouldn't lose much sleep over him, if I was you. Just go on about your own business."

A bolt of lightning lit up the sky. A limb split from a tree and crashed to the ground. We all looked over at the window. When it was quiet again, I said, "I told Ben he's welcome to come back to my cottage. I'm leaving for Boston in another week, but he could stay there until cold weather sets in. He'll need another place after that."

Jake took a long swig of beer, then picked at the label on his bottle. "Chrissakes," he said after a while, "got plenty of room right here. House is half-empty most of the time."

I jumped right in, leaning forward as I said, "It would be good for you to have Ben here. He could give you a hand with David."

Jake shot me a sharp look; I thought he was going to make some defensive remark. But he rubbed the gray bristles on his chin as he watched David dozing beside me on the floor. The wind made a long wailing cry as he admitted, "Guess I could use another pair of eyes to watch over him."

I settled back against the leg of the couch, a sense of relief rushing through me.

Jake said, "I'll be up front with you, Ben. I can't pay you a hell of a lot for working on the boat. Maybe we could work out a deal so some of your pay's in room and board."

"That'd be great," Ben said.

Jake looked down at his grown son, snoring and drooling, his head on my lap. "Ayuh, there's no two ways about it. Having another body here all the time would make me rest more easy."

"Do you think it'll bother David to have me around all the time?" Ben asked.

"He'll get used to it." Jake lifted his feet from the coffee table and planted them on the floor. "Well, that's enough of this foolishness. Sitting around in the dark, telling secrets like a bunch of women." He put his hands on his knees. "Jesus, what is this? Lights go out, and all of a sudden it's *Truth or Consequences* or some damn thing."

David's head lolled on my lap, and I began stroking his thin hair. He was sleeping soundly. "Sounds like the wind might be letting up some," I said. "Let's get an update on the weather."

"—headed out to sea," the staticky radio voice reported. "Winds are down to fifty-nine knots per hour. There are reports of trees uprooted in Rockland and Camden and some flooding in Thomaston, but most of Maine was spared damage. Rain is expected to get lighter but to continue all night, with partial clearing tomorrow . . ."

Just then the lights came back on. "Well, look at that. Guess I'll wake this boy and get him up to bed," Jake said, rising from his chair.

"Let me do it," Ben offered.

Jake seemed caught off guard, but then he sat back down. "It's all right by me. Might as well start earning your keep."

When Ben came back downstairs after helping David to bed, Jake said to him, "Go ahead and bunk down yourself. You can have that empty bedroom up there at the end of the hall. If that's okay with Martha—used to be hers when she was a girl."

"It's a nice room," I said. "There's plenty of space and a good view of the cove."

I took Ben upstairs to show him the room, then left him to get settled. Before I went back down, I stopped at David's room and set the flashlight on his dresser so he would have it in the morning. As I stood by his bed watching him sleep, I listened to the rain and wind outside, the bell buoy clanging in the cove. Strange, isn't it, I thought, how every day we face something unknown. As I pulled the bedspread up to his shoulders and wiped a string of drool from his chin, I thought, everything in life is a risk, including loving David. I turned to leave the room, then looked back at my nephew. His mouth was hanging open, he was snoring grossly, and his arms lay folded over his head like angel wings.

When I went downstairs, Jake was in the kitchen getting a fresh bottle of beer. "Boys settled in?" he asked.

I nodded and said, "I'm relieved Ben will be here to help out."

"No saying how long he'll stay. Young kid like that. What's he want with an old fart like me?"

"He's looking for a different kind of father."

"Well, I'm not gonna take the place of his old man, if that's what he's thinking. I got my hands full with David."

"You know, Jake, maybe that's something we should talk about. Someday you won't be here to look after David. Then what?"

"Oh, for chrissakes, don't go bringing that up!"

"Wait, hear me out. You're not getting any younger . . ."

"Jesus, Martha. You got me in a damn nursing home already. Look, that's neither here nor now, and I don't want to even think about it." Jake threw his head back and took a long swig of his beer.

There wasn't any use arguing with him. I started gathering my things, then tried calling Sue, but her line was down. "Jake, I'm going to call it a night. Looks like the worse of the storm is over."

He wiped beer foam from his lips with the back of his hand. "Might as well stay here till morning. You can sack out on the couch."

"Thanks, but I don't think so. I want to check on Sue and see if she's all right."

When I said goodnight, Jake patted my shoulder. "Take 'er easy," he said. "Roads are probably rutted pretty bad."

During the race from Jake's house to my car, I plunged right through a deep puddle and nearly slipped in the mud. I caught myself on my back fender to keep from falling, but water splashed up under my slicker. I was shivering as I started the car, and it took a while for the heater to kick in.

The wipers slapped rainwater back and forth across the windshield during the drive to the clinic. The wind had let up some, but I could see the damage it had done: bent trees along the side of the road, overturned lawn furniture in yards. I dashed from my car, ducking my head from the rain, and rapped loudly on Sue's front door. I don't think she heard me at first over the knocking of the wind, but after several more thumps with my fist the outside light came on and she cracked open the door.

"My God, Martha, are you crazy? It's a terrible night to be running around."

I quickly stepped into the house, and she pulled the door closed behind me. "I'm not running around," I said. "I came over to see if you were all right. I tried calling, but the phones aren't working."

"The storm must have knocked down the line. Come in, come in. Get out of those wet things." She pulled me into the hallway and began peeling off my slicker. Then she lifted off my hat, shook the water from it, and pointed to my boots. "Get out of those."

I kicked them off and stood in my stocking feet.

"God, even your clothes are wet. I'm drawing you a hot bath."

"Wait, you don't need to do that. I'll dry out."

"I'm already on my way to the tub," she called over her shoulder. "Make yourself at home."

In the living room, a warm fire was glowing orange in the brick fireplace. Sue must have been reading; a book lay face down on the floor by a chair. I glanced at it—*Women Who Run with the Wolves*. It was a paperback copy that I'd lent her a few years ago. I wondered why she was reading it now.

Having pulled off my wet socks, I was standing close to the fire, my arms wrapped around me, when she came into the room.

"Bath's ready."

"This isn't necessary, you know."

"Look at you. You're shivering. Go climb into the tub. I'll find a robe for you."

Sue had filled the tub with foamy bubble bath. The lights were dimmed, and five or six fat candles were burning. They gave off a wonderful scent of vanilla bean. I shrugged off my damp clothes and poked one foot gratefully into the tub. The water was almost too hot—just the way I liked it. Gingerly, I climbed in and inched deeper and deeper, my skin turning red.

I almost fell asleep in the tub. A discreet knocking at the bathroom door made me realize that quite a bit of time had passed. The tips of my fingers and toes were dimpled and shriveled from being submerged in the water so long.

"Martha, are you okay?" Sue called through the door.

"I'm fine," I laughed. "Just too lazy to get out and dry myself."

"Need some help?" Sue opened the door a crack and stuck her head in. The candles had burned down, wax pooling in their ceramic dishes, and the wonderful scent of vanilla drifted in the room. Sue lifted a large terry cloth towel from the rack and held it out for me. "Here," she said.

A little embarrassed, I climbed out of the tub, dripping onto the thick floor mat. From behind, she placed the towel over me like a cape, sponging the water drops from my body. Then she moved back and began rubbing my shoulders with it, vigorously wiping my skin. She toweled my spine, the small of my back, the backsides of my arms. Then she knelt and rubbed the backs of my legs. "There, turn around," she said as she finished drying my calves. Slowly I turned and faced her, my arms hanging awkwardly at my sides. When she looked up at me, I felt myself blush.

Sue stood, wrapped the now-damp towel around me, and pulled me to her. She held me, pressed tightly to her. I rested my head on her shoulder, taking in her heat. "I'm going to get you all wet," I whispered.

She squeezed me, then backed away. I tucked the edge of the terry cloth around my breasts, fashioning it into a sarong, as Sue took a smaller towel from the rack and began to scrub my hair. Closing my eyes, I thought of Grace and how I used to wash her hair and dry it with a heated towel.

"Put this on." Sue handed me a purple fleece robe.

I slipped my arms into it as she held it, then pulled the belt around my waist. "Umm, comfy," I said.

"Good. I don't have any extra slippers, so I brought these." Sue handed me a pair of heavy wool socks, gray with a red band around the top and at the heel. "They're not very glamorous, but they're warm."

I sat on the edge of the tub and pulled them onto my feet while Sue balled up the wet towels and dropped them into the laundry chute. "I feel much better," I said. "Thanks."

Sue yanked the plug in the tub. As the water drained, she blew out the candles, all except one. That one she picked up, carrying it by the ceramic plate it sat on. "Come out by the fire. I've got some hot cider waiting for you."

We settled in front of the fireplace, sitting next to each other on a lush fake fur rug. I held the mug of hot cider and stirred it with a cinnamon stick. "I didn't realize how tired I was. What a night I've had," I sighed. "As far as that goes, what a summer it's been."

Sue lay down on the rug, her face propped in her palms. The glow from the fire danced on her face. "Tell me about it," she said.

And I did. Finally. I told her everything. All the details. That David had grabbed at Grace and made her fall. That Jake had kept it a secret from me. That, when I found out, I'd shut them

both out of my life, unable to forgive either of them. And finally, that when Ben rescued David, I'd had a small glimmer of
understanding—a small realization of how vulnerable David is.

She listened carefully. When I was finished she said,
"You were going through all that and you didn't tell anyone? Why didn't you come to me?"

I didn't answer.

Sue put her hand on my ankle. "Why, Martha? Don't
you trust me?"

"Oh, that's not it. I just didn't think I should tell anyone.
And I was afraid that if you knew it might put you in a bad
spot. You might have to make a report or something."

"A report? To whom?"

"I don't know. Sheriff Clancy or someone. The medical
examiner? I really don't know." I added, "Sue, I only know
that Jake is terrified of people finding out. He's scared to
death that some one will take David away."

"I don't think that's going to happen. It's not like David
threw Grace overboard or hit her or anything. It really was
an accident, wasn't it?"

Again I didn't answer.

"Martha, it was . . . Just an accident."

"I guess," I said. Then I was crying, the tears just
streaming down my face.

Sue set her cup on the hearth, then set mine beside it.
After wiping my cheeks with a tissue, she shifted closer to
me, took both my hands and held them in her lap. "I can't
even imagine how painful all this has been for you," she
said, looking into my eyes. "Losing Grace. I know how
much you loved each other."

I could only nod.

Again Sue wiped my cheeks, and then she pulled me to
her. "Let it out," she whispered. "Let it go."

I sobbed into her neck until I was limp and cried out. After I quieted down, Sue got up to stoke the fire, adding two big logs to the flames. When she sat back down, she began gently kneading my shoulders.

Patting her hands, I said, "I'm better now. No more of this damn sniffling, I promise."

"Hey, it's all right."

"I feel like such a baby."

"Don't be silly," Sue said. "You're still dealing with grief. Be gentle on yourself. Are you tired?"

"Um hum." A big yawn escaped from my lips.

"Here, stretch out. This rug is really soft. You can put your head in my lap."

This time I did fall asleep. I don't know how long I slept, but I came awake to find Sue stroking my hair. She had such a tender look on her face as she looked down at me. "What time is it?" I asked.

"Almost two a.m., according to the clock on the mantle."

"I really should get home," I said, but I didn't stir a muscle.

"Why go out again in the storm? You might as well stay the rest of the night." The fire had died down, and the candle had burned out. The room was getting chilly. "Come on," Sue said, standing and pulling me to my feet. "My bed will hold both of us."

In bed, we lay facing each other. She caressed my cheekbone, her fingers traced the hollow of my neck. I didn't realize how hungry I was for the soft touch of another woman. All it took was that one touch, and I felt myself melting. Then I was swept with guilt, feeling disloyal to Grace. "Wait, Sue," I whispered. "I don't know if this is right. Grace . . . ."

"She's gone now, Martha," she whispered into my ear.

"Don't shut yourself off. Grace would want you to find some happiness." Sue kissed me then, not like an old friend, but long and deep and probing like a lover. With the storm still moaning outside, I gave myself to her, and it seemed like the most natural thing in the world.

My cottage weathered the storm pretty well, but still it took a few days to clean up the mess: mopping up rainwater on the porch, replacing a cracked windowpane in the door, clearing away broken limbs around my property. After those jobs were done, I got the cottage ready to be closed up for winter. As I packed, I took down the photos of Grace from my bedroom walls and added them to the suitcase for my city apartment.

The day before I planned to leave, I stopped by Jake's to say goodbye. "How much damage did you get from the storm?" I asked him.

"*The Sybil* stood up to the wind real good," he said. "Had a little bit of water in her, but the bilge pump kept her in pretty good shape. I got the rest of it mopped up. The radio antenna's bent and the window in the wheelhouse is busted, but I can get those fixed easy enough."

I told him I'd be leaving for Boston in the morning, and he said he'd keep an eye on my cottage for me. David gave me a big bear hug and a sloppy kiss on the cheek. Ben had gone into the village, so I didn't get a chance to say a proper goodbye to him.

There was one thing left to do before I headed for Boston. As I climbed Middle Hill, I grew winded. The path was overgrown, and dying grasses, black-eyed susan, coneflower brushed against my legs. When I came to the old cemetery, I opened the gate and went inside. Drawn to the ancient headstones covered with lichen, I read names and dates: *Helen Thayer, wife and mother, 1873-1924. Baby Thayer, 1890-1891. Clayton Drawbridge, rest in peace, 1846-1912.*

As I walked around, looking at headstones that leaned in the tall grass, I realized this was the cemetery Ben had visited. Where he'd come those nights earlier in the summer when he'd been planning his own death. I shuddered to think how close he'd come to carrying that out.

I adjusted the knapsack on my back, closed the rusted iron gate, and continued my walk. At the end of every season, Grace and I had climbed Middle Hill to say goodbye to the island, and it seemed like the right thing to do now. Near the top, I turned and scanned the bay below. Everything looked smaller from up here.

I swung the canvas knapsack from my back. With a collapsible spade, I dug a hole and lined it with moss. I lifted the engraved rosewood box from the knapsack and unhooked the latch. With my hand, I scooped out some of Grace's ashes. They felt light and heavy at the same time, fine as dust mixed with bone. "Rest now, dearest." I dropped that handful and most of the rest of her ashes into the hole, covered them with earth, and used stones flecked with mica to mark the little grave.

From the bay below, the horn of the ferry bleated. I chose one of the mica stones, broke a twig from a nearby spruce tree, picked up a downy gull feather, and put all these into the rosewood box over the powdery layer of ashes that remained. I slipped the box into the knapsack, then swung the pack over my shoulders and started back down the hill.

On the ferry, I parked in the bow and climbed the companionway to the top deck. I spotted Jake down below on the landing, and he gave me a thumbs-up. David smiled and tried to wink at me, but closed both eyes. Ben stood quietly behind them.

As the boat revved its motor, I saw Sue running across the parking lot. She came to a stop on the dock and called up to me. "Do you want me to come to Boston to see you?"

I cupped my mouth and yelled over the sound of the motor. "Yes. Soon!" As the ferry pulled slowly from the dock, I waved to her and she blew me a kiss.

The boat plowed through The Reach, and I had a clear view of Old Cove, *The Sybil* on its mooring, Jake's house in the meadow. I took one last look at my cottage on the cliff at Seal Point. Then I turned my attention forward; behind me Quarry Island grew slowly smaller.

There was a slight chop on the water, and sun shone through a gap in the clouds. Underneath my fisherman's sweater, I wore Grace's pendant on the chain around my neck. As the ferry pounded across the expanse of sea, I felt the smooth skin of the pearl bouncing against my chest, near my heart.

ABOUT THE AUTHOR

Laurel Mills grew up close to ocean waves in Maine and now lives near waving wheat fields in the Midwest. She earned a bachelor's degree in English and master's degree in Humanities from the University of Wisconsin-Oshkosh. She is editor of the literary magazine *Fox Cry Review* and Lecturer in English at the University of Wisconsin-Fox Valley.

Mills has been a successful poet for many years; most recently her work appeared in *Boomer Girls: Poems by Women from the Baby Boom Generation* (University of Iowa Press). Her poems have been published in various magazines, including *Ms., Yankee, Sinister Wisdom* and *Calyx.*

Her four award-winning collections of poems can be found on amazon.com. *I Sing Back* (Black Hat Press) won the Pippistrelle Best of Small Press Award. *Troika IV: Hidden Seed* (Thorntree Press) earned the Posner Poetry Award. *Canada Geese Coming Home* (Wolfinger Press) received an award from the Council for Wisconsin Writers Award. *The Gull is My Divining Rod* (Wisconsin Review Press) was awarded Wisconsin Library Association's Outstanding Achievement Honors.

In collaboration with composer Julie Gardner Bray, Mills composed the lyrics for *Be the Stream That Oxbows* (Heritage Music Press) and *When Blackberries Come Again* (Boosey & Hawkes, Inc.)

Mills was awarded writing residencies at Ragdale Foundation in Lake Forest, Illinois, where she completed much of the work on *Undercurrents,* her first full-length novel. She is currently working on a second novel, *Hurricane Mountain,* set in the low mountains of western Maine.

She and her partner Lynn live in Neenah, Wisconsin, where they raised two daughters and a son. Both in their mid-fifties, they are now re-visiting motherhood and raising their orphaned ten-year-old nephew.

For more great titles from Rising Tide Press,
please check out our website.

*We are committed to our community and
welcome your comments.*

We can be reached at our website:
www.risingtidepress.com

More Fiction to Stir the Imagination
From Rising Tide Press

CLOUD NINE AFFAIR   Katherine E. Kreuter
Christine Grandy—rebellious, wealthy, twenty-something—has disappeared, along with her lover Monica Ward. Desperate to bring her home, Christine's millionaire father hires Paige Taylor. But the trail to Christine is mined with obstacles, while powerful enemies plot to eliminate her. Eventually, Paige discovers that this mission is far more dangerous than she dreamed. A witty, sophisticated mystery by the best-selling author of Fool Me Once, filled with colorful characters, plot twists, and romance. $11.99

THE DEPOSITION   Katherine E. Kreuter
It is April in Paris and the Deposition's loopy narrator, G.B. is plotting the caper of capers. This provocative and hilarious novel by the author of the Paige Taylor Mystery Series resonates with gasps and guffaws. $12.00

STORM RISING   Linda Kay Silva
The excitement continues in this wonderful continuation of TROPICAL STORM. Join Megan and Connie as they set out to find Delta and bring her home. The meaning of friendship and love is explored as Delta, Connie, Megan and friends struggle to stay alive and stop General Zahn. Again the Costa Rican Rain Forest is the setting for another fast-paced action adventure. Storm fans won't want to miss this next installment in the Delta Stevens Mystery Series. $12.00

TROPICAL STORM   Linda Kay Silva
Another winning, action-packed adventure featuring smart and sassy heroines, an exotic jungle setting, and a plot with more twists and turns than a coiled cobra. Megan has disappeared into the Costa Rican rain forest and it's up to Delta and Connie to find her. Can they reach Megan before it's too late? Will Storm risk everything to save the woman she loves? Fast-paced, full of wonderful characters and surprises. Not to be missed. $11.99

CALLED TO KILL   Joan Albarella
Nikki Barnes, Reverend, teacher and Vietnam Vet is once again entangled in a complex web of murder and drugs when her past collides with the present. Set in the rainy spring of Buffalo, Dr. Ginni Clayton and her friend Magpie add spice and romance as Nikki tries to solve the mystery that puts her own life in danger. A fun and exciting read. $12.00

AGENDA FOR MURDER   Joan Albarella
A compelling mystery about the legacies of love and war, set on a sleepy college campus. Though haunted by memories of her tour of duty in Vietnam, Nikki Barnes is finally putting back the pieces of her life, only to collide with murder and betrayal. $11.99

ONE SUMMER NIGHT   Gerri Hill
Johanna Marshall doesn't usually fall into bed with someone she just met, but Kelly Sambino isn't just anyone. Hurt by love and labeled a womanizer, can these two women learn to trust one another and let love find its way? $12.00

BY THE SEA SHORE   Sandra Morris (avail 10/00)
A quiet retreat turns into more investigative work for Jess Shore in the summer town of Provincetown, MA. This page-turner mystery will keep you entertained as Jess struggles with her individuality while solving an attempted murder case. $12.00

AND LOVE CAME CALLING   Beverly Shearer
A beautifully told love story as old as time, steeped in the atmosphere of the Old West. Danger lights the fire of passion between two women whose lives become entwined when Kendra (Kenny), on the run from the law, happily stumbles upon the solitary cabin where Sophie has been hiding from her own past. Together, they learn that love can overcome all obstacles. $11.99

SIDE DISH   Kim Taylor
A genuinely funny yet tender novel which follows the escapades of Muriel, a twenty-something burmed—out waitress with a college degree, who has turned gay slacker living into an art form. Getting by on margaritas and old movies, she seems to have resigned herself to low standards, simple pleasures, and erotic daydreams. But in secret, Muriel is searching for true love. $11.99

COMING ATTRACTIONS
Bobbi D. Marolt

Helen Townsend reluctantly admits she's tried of being lonely...and of being closeted. Enter Princess Charming in the form of Cory Chamberlain, a gifted concert pianist. And Helen embraces joy once again. But can two women find happiness when one yearns to break out of the closet and breathe free, while the other fears that it will destroy her career? A delicious blend of humor, heart and passion—a novel that captures the bliss and blundering of love.
$11.99

ROUGH JUSTICE
Claire Youmans

When Glenn Lowry's sunken fishing boat turns up four years after its disappearance, foul play is suspected. Classy, ambitious Prosecutor Janet Schilling immediately launches a murder investigation, which produces several surprising suspects-one of them, her own former lover Catherine Adams, now living a reclusive life on an island. A real page-turner!
$10.99

NO CORPSE
Nancy Sanra

The third Tally McGinnis mystery is set aboard an Olivia Cruise. Tally and Katie thought they were headed out for some sun and fun. Instead, Tally finds herself drawn into a reunion cruise gone awry. When women start turning up dead, it is up to Tally and Cid to find the murderer and unravel a decades old mystery. Sanra fans new and old, won't be disappointed.
$12.00

NO ESCAPE
Nancy Sanra

This edgy, fast-paced whodunit set in picturesque San Francisco, will keep you guessing. Lesbian PI Tally McGinnis is called into action when Dr. Rebecca Toliver is charged with the murder of her lover Melinda. Is the red rose left at the scene the crime the signature of a copycat killer, or is the infamous Marcia Cox back, and up to her old, evil tricks again?
$11.99

NO WITNESSES
Nancy Sanra

This cliffhanger of a mystery set in San Francisco, introduces Detective Tally McGinnis, whose ex-lover Pamela Tresdale is arrested for the grisly murder of a wealthy Texas heiress. Tally rushes to the rescue despite friends' warnings, and is drawn once again into Pamela's web of deception and betrayal as she attempts to clear her and find the real killer.
$9.99

DEADLY RENDEZVOUS
Diane Davidson

A string of brutal murders in the middle of the desert plunges Lt. Toni Underwood and her lover Megan into a high profile investigation, which uncovers a world of drugs, corruption and murder, as well as the dark side of the human mind. Explosive, fast-paced, & action-packed.
$9.99

DEADLY GAMBLE
Diane Davidson

Las-Vegas-city of bright lights and dark secrets-is the perfect setting for this intriguing sequel to DEADLY RENDEZVOUS. Former police detective Toni Underwood and her partner Sally Murphy are catapulted back into the world of crime by a letter from Toni's favorite aunt. Now a prominent madam, Vera Valentine fears she is about to me murdered-a distinct possibility.
$11.99

RETURN TO ISIS
Jean Stewart

It is the year 2093, and Whit, a bold woman warrior from an Amazon nation, rescues Amelia from a dismal world where females are either breeders or drones. During their arduous journey back to the shining all-women's world of Artemis, they are unexpectedly drawn to each other. This engaging first book in the series has it all-romance, mystery, and adventure.
$9.99

ISIS RISING
Jean Stewart

In this stirring romantic fantasy, the familiar cast of lovable characters begins to rebuild the colony of Isis, burned to the ground ten years earlier by the dread Regulators. But evil forces threaten to destroy their dream. A swashbuckling futuristic adventure and an endearing love story all rolled into one.
$11.99

WARRIORS OF ISIS
Jean Stewart

The third lusty tale is one of high adventure and passionate romance among the Freeland Warriors. Arinna Sojourner, the evil product of genetic engineering, vows to destroy the fledgling colony of Isis with her incredible psychic powers. Whit, Kali, and other warriors battle to save their world, in this novel bursting with life, love, heroines and villains. *A Lambda Literary Award Finalist*
$11.99

EMERALD CITY BLUES
Jean Stewart

When comfortable yuppie world of Chris Olson and Jennifer Hart collides with the desperate lives of Reb and Flynn, two lesbian runaways struggling to survive on the streets of Seattle, the forecast is trouble. A gritty, enormously readable novel of contemporary lesbigay life, which raises real questions about the meaning of family and community. This book is an excellent choice for young adults and the more mature reader.
$11.99

DANGER IN HIGH PLACES   Sharon Gilligan
Set against the backdrop of Washington, D.C., this riveting mystery introduces freelance photographer and amateur sleuth, Alix Nicholson. Alix stumbles on a deadly scheme, and with the help of a lesbian congressional aide, unravels the mystery.   **$9.99**

DANGER! CROSS CURRENTS   Sharon Gilligan
The exciting sequel to Danger in High Places brings freelance photographer Alix Nicholson face-to-face with an old love and a murder. When Alix's landlady turns up dead, and her much younger lover, Leah Claire, the prime suspect, Alix launches a frantic campaign to find the real killer.   **$9.99**

HEARTSONE AND SABER   Jacqui Singleton
You can almost hear the sabers clash in this rousing tale of good and evil, of passionate love between a bold warrior queen and a beautiful healer with magical powers.   **$10.99**

PLAYING FOR KEEPS   Stevie Rios
In this sparkling tale of love and adventure, Lindsay West an oboist, travels to Caracas, where she meets three people who change her life forever: Rob Heron a gay man, who becomes her dearest friend; her lover Mercedes Luego, a lovely cellist, who takes Lindsay on a life-altering adventure down the Amazon; and the mysterious jungle-dwelling woman Arminta, who touches their souls.   **$10.99**

LOVESPELL   Karen Williams
A deliciously erotic and humorous love story in which Kate Gallagher, a shy veterinarian, and Allegra, who has magic at her fingertips, fall in love. A masterful blend of fantasy and reality, this beautifully written story will delight your heart and imagination.   **$12.00**

NIGHTSHADE   Karen Williams
Alex Spherris finds herself the new owner of a magical bell, which some people would kill for. She is ushered into a strange & wonderful world and meets Orielle, who melts her frozen heart. A heart-warming romance spun in the best tradition of storytelling.   **$11.99**

FEATHERING YOUR NEST:
An Interactive Workbook& Guide to a Loving Lesbian Relationship
                Gwen Leonhard, M.ED./Jennie Mast, MSW
This fresh, insightful guide and workbook for lesbian couples provides effective ways to build and nourish your relationships. Includes fun exercises & creative ways to spark romance, solve conflict, fight fair, conquer boredom, spice up your sex lives.   **$14.99**

SHADOWS AFTER DARK   Ouida Crozier
While wings of death are spreading over her own world, Kyril is sent to earth to find the cure. Here, she meets the beautiful but lonely Kathryn, and they fall deeply in love. But gradually, Kathryn learns that her exotic new lover has been sent to earth with a purpose—to save her own dying vampire world. A tender, finely written story.   **$9.95**

SWEET BITTER LOVE   Rita Schiano
Susan Fredrickson is a woman of fire and ice—a successful high-powered executive, she is by turns sexy and aloof. From the moment writer Jenny Ceretti spots her at the Village Coffeehouse, her serene life begins to change. As their friendship explodes into a blazing love affair, Jenny discovers that all is not as it appears, while Susan is haunted by ghosts from a past that won't stay hidden. A roller-coaster romance which vividly captures the rhythm and feel of love's sometimes rocky ride and the beauty of life after recovery.   **$10.99**

UNDERCURRENTS   Laurel Mills
Photographer Martha Felkins returns for the summer to the rugged Maine island where she grew up. It has been nine months since her companion Grace died here in a strange accident on *The Sybil*, a lobster boat captained by Martha's brother. Martha has come back, hoping that being near her brother and his grown retarded son will help her heal from grief. Instead, she uncovers the shocking secret behind Grace's fatal accident (a secret even the island doctor, Sue Whitaker, doesn't know).   **$13.99**

HOW TO ORDER

TITLE	AUTHOR	PRICE
☐ Agenda for Murder	Joan Albarella	11.99
☐ And Love Came Calling	Beverly Shearer	11.99
☐ Called to Kill	Joan Albarella	12.00
☐ Cloud Nine Affair	Katherine Kreuter	11.99
☐ Coming Attractions	Bobbi D. Marolt	11.99
☐ Danger! Cross Currents	Sharon Gilligan	9.99
☐ Danger in High Places	Sharon Gilligan	9.95
☐ Deadly Gamble	Diane Davidson	11.99
☐ Deadly Rendezvous	Diane Davidson	9.99
☐ Dreamcatcher	Lori Byrd	9.99
☐ Emerald City Blues	Jean Stewart	11.99
☐ Feathering Your Nest	Leonhard/Mast	14.99
☐ Heartstone and Saber	Jaqui Singleton	10.99
☐ Isis Rising	Jean Stewart	11.99
☐ Lovespell	Karen Williams	12.00
☐ Nightshade	Karen Williams	11.99
☐ No Escape	Nancy Sanra	11.99
☐ No Witness	Nancy Sanra	11.99
☐ No Corpse	Nancy Sanra	12.00
☐ One Summer Night	Gerri Hill	12.00
☐ Playing for Keeps	Stevie Rios	10.99
☐ Return to Isis	Jean Stewart	9.99
☐ Rough Justice	Claire Youmans	10.99
☐ Shadows After Dark	Ouida Crozier	9.95
☐ Side Dish	Kim Taylor	11.99
☐ Storm Rising	Linda Kay Silva	12.00
☐ Sweet Bitter Love	Rita Schiano	10.99
☐ The Deposition	Katherine Kreuter	12.00
☐ Tropical Storm	Linda Kay Silva	11.99
☐ Undercurrents	Laurel Mills	13.99
☐ Warriors of Isis	Jean Stewart	11.99

Please send me the books I have checked. I enclosed a check or money order, plus $4 for the first book and $1 for each additional book to cover shipping and handling.

Name (please print) _____

Address: _____

_____

City: _____ State: _____ Zip: _____

Arizona residents please add 7.6% sales tax to total.

Send to: Rising Tide Press
PO Box 30457, Tucson, Arizona 85751

Or visit our website: www.risingtidepress.com